Forbidden Island
The Mystery Club 3

Fiona Kelly

KNIGHT BOOKS
Hodder and Stoughton

Copyright © by Ben M. Baglio 1993

Created by Ben M. Baglio
London W12 7HG

First published in Great Britain in 1993 by Knight Books

Printed and bound in Great Britain for Hodder and Stoughton Children's Books, a division of Hodder and Stoughton Ltd, Mill Road, Dunton Green, Sevenoaks, Kent TN13 2YA (Editorial Office: 47 Bedford Square, London WC1B 3DP) by Cox & Wyman Ltd, Reading, Berks. Typeset by Hewer Text Composition Services, Edinburgh.

A Catalogue record for this book is available from the British Library

ISBN 0 340 58869 1

To the memory of Mary Ross

1 Mysterious lights

'OK girls,' Mr Adams said as he pulled in to the kerb. 'This is it. Out you get.' He looked across at Holly. 'Apologise to your aunt for me. Tell her I can't stay. I've got an appointment to see a client at four o'clock. And, Holly . . .'

'Yes, Dad?'

'Try not to get yourself involved in any more scrapes, do you mind?'

Holly's eyes widened. 'Me? I don't get myself involved. It just happens.'

Mr Adams gave a wry smile. 'Holly, you attract trouble like a magnet. Will you try – just for this week?' He heaved a mock sigh. 'Carole didn't know what she was letting herself in for when she said she'd take you three for the holidays.'

'Don't worry, Mr Adams,' said Belinda. 'I, for one, don't intend to do anything more exciting than lying on the beach. I'll keep them under control. Trust me.'

Mr Adams laughed. He knew it was unlikely Belinda would be able to control his lively fifteen-year-old daughter. It would be like a snail trying to control a grasshopper. 'Right. Have a good time, then. See you next week.'

The three girls got their bags out of the back of the car and waved him goodbye. Tall and pretty in a blue striped tracksuit, Holly walked briskly up the path, her light brown hair bouncing in the breeze.

'Hang on a minute.' Tracy stopped to tuck her violin case more securely under her arm, then shifting her sports bag over to her other hand, she caught up with her friend in a couple of strides.

As usual, Belinda brought up the rear. Polishing her spectacles on the sleeve of her faded green sweatshirt, she picked up her case and trailed along behind them. She reached the front door just as Holly rang the bell for the second time.

'Try again,' Tracy suggested after a few moments without a reply.

Belinda shook her head. 'No point. She's got a car, hasn't she?'

'A car? Yes. Why?' Holly's grey eyes were puzzled.

'Look at the garage. No way could she keep a car in there. It's falling apart. And no car in the drive. So, she must be out.'

Holly and Tracy exchanged glances. There were times when Belinda seemed to hit the nail on the head without even trying.

'OK, Miss Private Eye,' Tracy kidded, 'what now?'

Belinda shrugged. 'Don't ask me. It's Holly's aunt.'

'Let's go round the back. She may have left a note or something,' Tracy suggested.

But the back of the house was securely locked up, and there was no sign of a note anywhere.

Holly frowned. 'That's weird. She knew we were coming. You'd think she'd be here.'

'Perhaps she's gone out to get some bread or something,' Tracy said.

Holly shook her head. 'More likely to have gone to see a house.'

'A house?'

'She's an estate agent. She used to be in a big office in York, but now she's got her own business here in Framley. I expect someone rang up and she didn't want to leave it till tomorrow in case the other agency gets it. There's only the two of them in Framley and the competition's really keen.'

'There's a window open upstairs,' Tracy said.

Belinda dumped her bag and sprawled out on one of the patio chairs. 'Well, you two can do what you like. I'm going to relax.' She took a Mars bar out of her bag and, tilting her head up to the warm sunshine, took a bite.

Holly and Tracy looked up at the window. It was only slightly ajar, but maybe they could reach it.

Tracy tugged at a tangle of branches that snaked their way up the wall and across a tiny balcony beneath the window. 'Think this will hold me?'

'Looks a bit brittle,' Holly said warily.

'I'm going to try.' Tracy grabbed at the trunk. The sun glinted for a moment on her short blonde hair. Then she disappeared into the canopy of leaves. Seconds later there was an ominous creaking noise and a length of tree pulled away from the wall.

'Whoops! I knew we shouldn't have had those chocolate éclairs on the drive over here,' Tracy giggled.

'Be careful,' Holly said. 'It may be one of Aunt Carole's prize plants.'

From her vantage point above them, Tracy looked around. 'Judging by the state of the garden, she's got too many prize plants. You couldn't fit another in anywhere. Anyway, which do you care more about – her prize plants or your best friend's life?'

'Get on with it.' Holly grinned.

A few minutes later Tracy was on the balcony, and from there it didn't take long to get the window open and climb inside. 'I won't be long,' she called down. 'Meet you at the front porch.'

When the door opened, Tracy looked impressed. 'This place is bigger than it looks. And the view . . . You can see for miles. There's an island in the bay. Think we could hire a boat and have a look?'

Holly pushed past her. 'I doubt it. Aunt Carole

told me it's not allowed. I don't know why.'

'Well, there's someone there now. I saw lights flashing.'

'Probably just the sun reflecting off some glass or something. Anyway, now we're here I'll show you the bedrooms.'

Belinda and Tracy followed Holly up the two flights of stairs to what had once been the servants' quarters. In contrast to the spaciousness of her aunt's room on the first floor, all three bedrooms on this level were tiny, with sloping ceilings and windows that jutted out into the roof. But they were fully fitted, and furnished in bold, dramatic colours, each with its own washbasin. There was also a bathroom and shower as well as a tiny sitting-room with television and stereo all on the same level.

'Fantastic,' Tracy said admiringly. 'It's just like having your own apartment. If this was my family I'd be down here every weekend.'

Just then, they heard the crunch of tyres on gravel and the slam of a car door. 'That'll be her,' Holly said. 'Come on.'

They ran downstairs, and were in the hall as Aunt Carole opened the door.

'I'm so sorry, girls,' she said. 'I meant to be home ages ago, but I got delayed.'

'You didn't mind us coming in before you got home, did you?' Holly asked.

11

'Of course not.' She looked vaguely round, as if she'd lost something. Holly noticed that her hands were shaking, and that there two high spots of colour in her cheeks, as if she had been having a furious row. *Strange*, thought Holly. *Aunt Carole is usually so cool and laid back.*

'You haven't met my friends,' Holly said. 'This is Belinda Hayes. And this is Tracy Foster. She's half American. I wrote to you about them, when I started the Mystery Club.'

'Hi.' Tracy smiled, but Aunt Carole didn't seem to notice.

'Sorry. I've had a bad day. Let me have a shower and change, then I'll be human again. Help yourself to whatever you want in the fridge. I'll be back.'

Belinda and Tracy exchanged glances as she hurried past and up the stairs.

Holly's cheeks reddened. She tried to cover up her embarrassment. 'Like she said, she's had a bad day. Oh, well, let's see what there is to eat.'

By the time Aunt Carole reappeared they had made some toasted sandwiches and were sitting in front of the TV.

'That's better,' she said. 'Sorry I was so prickly before. I had a bit of a brush with another estate agent.'

Within minutes they were laughing and chatting

12

together, the earlier awkwardness forgotten. 'So, Holly . . . tell me about the Mystery Club.'

Holly's eyes glowed. There was nothing she liked better than talking about the Mystery Club. 'Well, you know how lonely I was when we first moved to Willow Vale? I didn't know anyone there, and it's really difficult starting in a new school right in the middle of a school year . . .'

Her aunt nodded sympathetically.

'Anyway, I put an advert in the school newspaper to see if anyone else was interested in mystery stories. And these two turned up.'

She grinned round at Tracy and Belinda. 'They didn't know much about mysteries when we started – well, none of us did, in a way. But you'd be surprised what's turned up since then.'

'So your father tells me,' Aunt Carole said dryly. 'Some of them more exciting than you expected, I gather.'

Holly smiled. 'A bit,' she admitted.

Carole turned to Tracy. 'And you're from America, Holly says.'

'Yeah, California. But I've been in England since I was twelve. I came back with Mom when my parents got divorced. We've lived in Willow Vale ever since.'

'She's brilliant at virtually everything. Games . . . music . . . You name it and she can do it,' Holly put in. 'I reckon she'll be in the Olympics one day.'

13

Tracy reddened. 'Don't believe her, Miss Earnshaw. Holly's practising to be a journalist. And if she can't find interesting facts to write about she makes them up as she goes along.'

Aunt Carole laughed. 'She's always been the same. That's what makes her so good at detective work. By the way, I've got a copy of a new mystery novel for you, Holly. Are you interested?'

'You bet! Thanks.'

'And, girls . . . skip the Miss Earnshaw bit. I'm Carole, right?'

'Right.'

They had just finished the evening meal and were clearing the dishes into the kitchen when a car's headlights swept the windows. Seconds later, the doorbell rang furiously.

Carole was in the middle of loading the dishwasher. Before she had time to go to the door, the bell rang again.

Holly raised an eyebrow. *Someone* was in a hurry. 'Go ahead,' she said. 'We'll finish off here.'

Hastily the three friends cleared the rest of the table, listening with unease at the raised voices in the hallway. Then, as Holly took out the last few plates, the living-room door burst open and a tall, heavily-built man in his mid-thirties strode into the room.

14

Ignoring Holly completely, he turned to face Carole who had followed him in. 'And another thing,' he continued, 'Wetherby's Farm is *our* market property. Don't think you can muscle in and take our custom.'

'Mr Hare,' Carole replied coolly, 'don't rush to conclusions. I didn't "muscle in". That property has been on the market for six months, and what have you done about it? Nothing. This afternoon Mrs Wetherby phoned me and I went there to value it. You can't expect her to sit around and wait for you forever. If I can't do better than you I'll eat my hat!'

You tell him, Holly thought.

'You're a newcomer here,' he snarled. 'You've only been in Framley for six months. Bingley and Hare have been here for sixty years.'

'Oh, really?' Carole replied sweetly. 'I didn't think you were that old.'

The man's colour deepened. He looked as if he would explode at any minute.

Holly took out the plates, and leaned against the kitchen door, grinning.

'No need to worry about Carole,' she said. 'She's an expert at putting people in their place.'

By the time they had finished loading the dishwasher and clearing up the kitchen, the man had left.

'All clear,' Carole said, popping her head round

the door. 'Thank you for taking over. Now we can have our coffee in peace.'

'What was all that about?' asked Holly, as she took in the coffee on a tray.

'That's Mr High-and-Mighty Hare. Junior partner in the only other estate agency in Framley. Old Mr Bingley's all right. I get on well with him, but he's more or less retired. He only comes in a couple of times a week. This one thinks he owns the place.' She sighed. 'I won't go into details. I've just got a weird feeling that there's more to this set-up than meets the eye.'

'Tell us,' said Holly, intrigued.

Her aunt hesitated. 'It doesn't sound much when you put it into words. It may not be anything, really. But somehow . . . when I went to see Mrs Wetherby at the farm today I felt as though something sinister was going on.' She paused again.

'Sinister? Why?' Holly's grey eyes sparkled. If there was anything to raise her interest it was the thought of something sinister going on.

'Well . . . Mrs Wetherby's a widow, and she's got a farm down on Fram Bight . . .'

'Fram *what*?' Tracy giggled. 'You English sure have got some funny names.'

'Not bite, as in B-I-T-E,' Carole laughed. 'Bight as in bend in the coast. It's where the land loops out into the sea. Anyway, it's an isolated place. Only

16

Framley Grange, the farm – and, of course, the island. Yet Mrs Wetherby is convinced that there are strange people hanging around. She said she's seen flashing lights in the night . . . tyres churning up the mud between the farm and the jetty . . . that sort of thing.' She sighed. 'I don't know how much is true and how much is her imagination. At her age it could be either.'

'I've seen the lights she's talking about,' Tracy said. 'They were coming from the island. This afternoon. When I climbed into your bedroom.'

Carole looked puzzled. 'That's impossible. No one's allowed on the island. It was used for experiments in germ warfare during the Second World War. Anthrax, I think. It's still lethal. You must have been mistaken. Perhaps it was a fishing boat in the bay.'

Holly was impatient to hear the rest of the story. 'Never mind about the lights. What else happened?'

'I told her to ring Bingley and Hare to let them know she had appointed me as her agent as well. Martyn Hare asked to speak to me, and he was really rude. Well, you heard him, so you can guess. Anyway, Mrs Wetherby is convinced that most of the things that are happening are to do with the new owners of Framley Grange. They're a couple of brothers, Thomas and Ian Clough. I thought I might pop in to see them in a day or two to see what it's all about.'

'Can we come?' Holly asked.

Carole shook her head. 'Sorry. Not for that sort of thing. I'll take you down there if you like. You can explore while I talk to them.'

They had to accept that for the time being, though Holly didn't like taking no for an answer. After all, why miss all the fun if there was some way of getting in on the act?

Before they went to bed that night, Holly called a meeting of the Mystery Club in the sitting-room upstairs. Moonlight filtered through the diamond-shaped panes of the window, patterning the carpet like a giant jigsaw, and the three sat in the glow of the gas-fire, talking.

'Why should that Martyn Hare be so miffed about Carole trying to sell the farm?' Holly mused. 'He's had six months to have a go.'

Belinda looked up from a copy of *Horse and Hound* that she'd found on the shelf. She was absolutely mad about everything to do with horses. 'Maybe he thinks women belong at home. Not at work, competing with men.'

Holly grinned. 'You could be right.'

'I wouldn't mind having a look at this Bight place tomorrow,' Tracy said. 'How far is it, Holly?'

'I'm not actually sure. I've only stayed here once

18

before – and that was when Mum and I came up for a couple of days to give Carole a hand to move in.'

'That explains it,' Tracy said. 'I wondered why you didn't say anything about the island and the germ warfare. It's a bit spooky, really. And what about the lights and things?'

'I think you're making a mystery out of nothing,' Belinda interrupted. 'There's probably a perfectly normal explanation. Anyway, I'm off to bed.' And tucking the magazine under her arm, she ambled out.

'Typical!' Tracy laughed. 'Give her a horse magazine, and you've lost her completely.'

But before Holly had a chance to comment, there was a shout from Belinda's room. 'Hey! Come and look. Quick!'

Holly and Tracy rushed into the other room. Belinda was standing by the window. The moon shone down out of a cloudless arch of sky. The island, a dark silhouette on the horizon, looked entirely deserted but for flickering shafts of light – white, then green, then white, then red.

And from the mainland came an answering signal. One . . . two . . . three green, and a longer flash of white.

2 Danger in the mist

Carole had gone to work by the time the girls came downstairs in the morning.

'I've been thinking,' Holly said. 'Those lights weren't anything to do with Morse code. We did Morse code in Guides. There are no colours involved, nor such long spaces between dots or dashes. But it was a message. I just wish I knew what it said.'

'It wasn't the same as I saw in the afternoon,' Tracy said. 'I didn't take much notice at the time, but I saw red lights – not green. And it wasn't a fishing boat. It wasn't any kind of boat.'

Belinda absent-mindedly put another piece of bread in the toaster. 'What I want to know is, if we can see them, why can't everyone else? Why isn't the whole town buzzing with rumours?'

'Perhaps it is,' said Holly.

'Can't be. Your aunt hasn't heard anything. An estate agent would be bound to pick up gossip. She'd need to in her job.'

'Perhaps you can't see the lights from the town,'

Holly mused. 'We're up much higher here. And Framley Bay is sort of round the corner from Framley itself.'

'But I saw them from her bedroom,' Tracy objected.

There was silence for a moment.

'That's true,' Holly said slowly. 'So why hasn't Carole seen them?'

There was only one way to find out. The three friends looked at one another. It was one thing to climb in through someone's bedroom window. It was quite another to go in deliberately just to look for something – even if it was only the view they were looking for.

The room was like Carole herself – cool and elegant. Furnished mainly in shades of white and grey, there were splashes of deep blue on cushions and lampshades. The whole of one wall was fitted wardrobes, a double bed took up most of another wall and a large dressing-table was angled across one corner of the set of windows which opened on to the tiny balcony.

Holly hesitated for a moment, then gave herself a mental shake. It had to be done. 'Where were you when you got in?' she asked Tracy.

Tracy went across the room. 'This is the window that was open,' she said, pointing across the mirror on the dressing-table to the window beyond.

'So you were behind the dressing-table?'

Tracy nodded.

Holly squeezed herself into the narrow triangle of space and looked out of the window.

'Tracy, you look out of the window from that end. Belinda, you face me, looking into the mirror. Right. Now, let's check . . .'

A few minutes later they had solved at least part of the puzzle.

Holly grinned triumphantly. 'You can see much further from here. But how often would anyone stand behind their dressing-table? They'd look in the mirror, or out of the window, or they'd wander round the room and catch a glimpse of what was going on outside but they wouldn't be *behind* the dressing-table, would they? I bet you can only see the lights from this very spot. And even then, you'd have to be here at the exact moment that the lights were flashing.'

'But we all saw them last night,' Tracy objected.

'We were upstairs. Another level higher,' Belinda reminded her. She turned to Holly with a delighted smile. '*That*'s why we could see the lights on the mainland. We were higher up.'

'OK, Sherlock Holmes!' Holly said. 'Now let's go and check out how much we can see from upstairs.'

They stood in Belinda's bedroom, looking out of the window. From here they could see a large house surrounded by trees with a thin spiral of

22

smoke coming from one of the chimneys. And way beyond that, a cottage and outbuildings stood on a loop of land that jutted out to sea.

'That must be Fram Bight,' Holly said. 'The big house will be the Grange, and the other one is probably Wetherby's Farm. The lights definitely came from that direction, and we're going to find out why. Come on, let's go.'

Belinda wrinkled her nose. 'I thought we were going to the beach. Can't we leave the Bight until tomorrow? It's miles away.'

But there was no way Holly was going to leave this mystery until it was solved. 'It won't be any nearer however long we wait,' she argued. 'We might just as well go today. Come on.' She led the way downstairs.

Belinda was still grumbling. 'Mum made me have a new swimsuit for this,' she said. 'She won't half go on at me if I don't even use it.'

'It's a wonder she didn't make you have a completely new outfit altogether,' Tracy teased. 'I bet she tried.'

Belinda gave a shamefaced smile. Her mother was always on at her to smarten herself up. Not that it made any difference. Although Belinda's family was rolling in money, Belinda always wore the same old jeans and faded green sweatshirt.

'We'll go to the beach tomorrow,' Holly said.

They made some cheese sandwiches and took a

few Cokes from the fridge. 'I don't suppose there'll be any shops up at the Bight,' Holly said. 'It looked pretty bleak.'

'Where do we catch the bus?' Belinda asked.

'Bus? To the Bight? You must be joking. I don't think Framley has caught on to buses yet,' said Holly.

Belinda squinted at them through her glasses. 'Do you mean we've got to walk all the way there *and* all the way back?'

'It will do you good,' Tracy said. 'Look at you. You're a mess. Time you lost some of that flab.'

'It's not flab,' Belinda said indignantly. 'I've got heavy bones.'

Tracy grinned. 'Have you heard the way your horse groans when you get on?'

Belinda flushed. She enjoyed her food and she wasn't going to give it up for anyone. But any suggestion that she wasn't treating her horse properly really made her mad. Meltdown was special. There was no way she'd do anything to hurt him.

'I'm not that heavy,' she defended herself. 'Meltdown could take twice my weight.' Then she grinned. 'You're winding me up,' she said. 'Why do I always fall for it?'

Carole's house was perched at the top of Tumble Avenue, a steep tree-lined road with about ten houses on either side, each standing in its own grounds. Some were sprawling, ranch-style buildings just one storey high, built around a courtyard or swimming pool. Others were taller, but faced a different direction. Of the three-storey houses, only Carole's faced the Bight.

No wonder no one has seen the lights, thought Holly. Carole's house was the last one in the avenue. From there on the road wound downhill in both directions.

'Come on,' she said confidently, though she wasn't at all sure whether they could reach the Bight that way or whether they would have to go back into Framley first.

By the time they reached the Esplanade, as it was grandly called, they seemed to have been walking downhill for ever. 'It'll be a long climb back,' Belinda said gloomily. 'And it looks like it's going to rain.'

'Rain? No way,' Holly laughed. 'If you collapse, we'll send a St Bernard out to look for you, with a bag of crisps and an ice cream fastened to its collar. That will get you home.'

It was a regular joke among the girls, that they'd do almost anything for an ice cream.

Belinda smiled. 'All right,' she said. 'Let's go.'

At the far end of the bay the road turned inland, with the gaps between houses growing wider and wider. At first, there were plenty of people about, but by the time they reached the Common a thick sea mist shrouded them in a veil of rain. There wasn't a soul to be seen. It felt like the last night of the world.

'Spooky,' Belinda said. 'Is it always like this?'

'How would I know?' Holly said, wishing they hadn't come after all. 'I've only been to Framley once before.'

They seemed to have left the road behind and were walking on scrubby moorland, the stubby grass crunching beneath their feet. There was no colour anywhere. The bushes, the grass, the sky, were all a leaden grey. Even the occasional glimpse of sun was like a silver ball hidden behind layers of grey gauze.

The only sounds they could hear were the pad of trainers on grass, and the swish of sea in the distance. It was scary. A shiver of gooseflesh ran up Holly's back.

'I saw a Miss Marple film like this,' Belinda said gloomily. 'I can't remember what it was called, but there was a mist, and the girl fell down a cliff and was killed. It turned out in the end that she'd taken out an insurance policy and her fiancé had pushed her over to get the money.'

'You *are* cheerful, aren't you?' Holly said. 'There are no cliffs here. And there's no insurance policy, no fiancé and no money. The only thing that's the same is the mist, and I'm soaked.'

'So am I,' Belinda complained. 'I told you it would rain. I wish we'd brought our anoraks.'

They plodded on. The mist grew thicker and thicker, swirling round them till they could see only a few metres in front of them.

'I hope we're not walking round in circles,' said Holly.

Suddenly, Tracy grabbed her arm with a shout of warning, and Holly saw that she was on the edge of a steep ravine.

'What did you say about there being no cliffs?' Tracy asked dryly.

Holly looked down at the shadowy blur of the choppy sea foaming at the rocks below. Her throat tightened. Another few steps and they would have been over the edge. 'You'd think there'd be a notice or something.'

'There is.' Belinda pointed at a board sticking out of the ground a few metres along the footpath. They moved up closer to read it.

DANGER – KEEP OUT
BY ORDER OF THE MINISTRY OF DEFENCE

Tracy edged past the notice towards the cliff.

'Don't!' Holly's voice was sharp with fear.

'I'm just looking.' Tracy peered over the edge. 'There's a couple of lengths of barbed-wire and concrete posts down there, with a whole lot of rock as well. There must have been a fall fairly recently.'

'We'll have to go back.' Holly swivelled round. Which direction had they come from? It all looked the same.

'We'll head inland,' she said. 'If we keep the sound of the sea behind us we can't go far wrong. The mist is bound to lift soon, or we'll come across a house or something.'

She shivered. Her T-shirt clung to her skin, and for once she envied Belinda's old green sweatshirt. At least that offered a bit more protection.

They hadn't gone far before they came across another board with a barbed-wire fence behind it. The message was the same, only this time it was on solid ground, overgrown with brambles and trees.

Holly breathed a sigh of relief. 'We'll follow the fence. It must come out somewhere.'

'Oh, yes?' Belinda's voice was sarcastic. 'And what if we find ourselves in the middle of a firing range? It does say "Ministry of Defence" you know.'

As if in answer to her remark, a rifle shot whistled past. Instinctively, all three dropped to the ground, their hearts pounding. Silence. They lay there for a couple of long minutes, afraid to move a muscle.

'That was close,' Holly said at last. 'You were right about the firing range.'

'Can't be,' Tracy said. 'There would have been a whole volley of shots, not just one.'

'Then who?' Holly cautiously got to her feet, ready to drop to the ground at the slightest sound. 'Do you suppose someone is shooting at us?'

'You said yourself it was a bit close. Why should someone who is inside Government land shoot towards the outside? It's dangerous. Anyone could be walking past. I reckon someone was trying to scare us off.'

'Well, whoever he is couldn't even see us in this fog,' Belinda said, dusting the twigs and grass off her jeans. 'It was just a mistake.'

Reassured, Holly said, 'Well, we can't stay here for ever. At least if we stick to the fence we won't walk over the cliff.'

Tracy grinned. 'Sure. Better to be shot than drowned.'

Keeping the fence as a marker they trudged through the wet grass for what seemed like hours. At last they were walking along a wide cart-track with high stone walls on either side. Holly felt her spirits rise. The track didn't look as if it was used very much, and it was rutted with mud, but at least it was a sign of civilisation.

'I wonder where we are?' she said.

'Heaven,' Tracy said with a laugh.

'No, seriously. I've no idea which way we've been walking for the last half-hour or so.'

'I don't either, but who cares? We're bound to come across something or someone soon – even if it's the man with the gun.'

A little further down the track they saw the bulky outline of a huge wrought-iron gate. 'There you are,' Tracy said. 'I told you we'd come across something soon.'

The gate was padlocked, but as they drew level they could see that it led to a gravelled drive winding between trees whose branches met overhead like a tunnel. A wooden board lay almost hidden by weeds in the ditch.

Holly bent down, clearing away the dirt with her hand so she could read it. Immediately a horde of woodlice scuttled off the board and into the tangle of brambles.

'Ugh!' She felt the hairs on the back of her neck rise. 'Horrible things.'

The gold paint was faded, the board cracked and eaten away in places. But there was no mistaking the name.

'Guess what?' she said. 'This is—'

But she got no further. Out of the shadows a large Alsatian appeared, barking furiously. He flung himself at the gate, rattling the padlock against the bars. And behind him loomed the figure of a man carrying a gun.

3   Hit and run

'Quiet, Prince.'

The dog's barking became a low growl as the man walked towards them.

'What d'you want?'

He made no attempt to open the gate, but spoke to them through the bars, his voice curt. He was average height with a craggy face and dark hair, receding slightly. Holly guessed he was about forty years old, though he could have been younger. It was one of those faces that could be almost any age.

Holly's pulse quickened. Was this the man who had shot at them? He was heavily built, and looked tough, but there was no threat at the moment. The gun was held casually in the crook of his arm. She relaxed a little.

'We're staying with my aunt. We got lost when the mist came down.'

'So what do you expect me to do?'

Holly stiffened. If this was one of the Clough brothers, no wonder Mrs Wetherby was having problems with them.

'If I could use your phone, I would like to ring my aunt, please. Then perhaps you could tell us the way back to Framley Bay? I'll give you the money to pay for the call,' she added coldly.

He looked them up and down for a moment. 'You'd better come in,' he said, unlocking the gate. Then, without waiting to see if they were following, he turned on his heel and led the way down the drive.

The three girls exchanged glances. Tracy made up her mind first, and pushed the gate open. The dog growled a warning.

'Prince!'

The dog padded after his master.

The Grange stood in a clearing, a bleak Victorian building that looked more like a prison than a house. A tractor stood in the yard, and behind it Holly could see the bonnet of a car protruding from a garage.

The man opened the front door, pushing the dog to one side with his boot. 'In there.'

There was a nameplate screwed to the door. 'CLOUGH BROS. SCRAP DEALERS'. Scrap dealers? What were scrap dealers doing in such an isolated place? Holly wondered.

'Ian!' His voice echoed round the bare hall.

'Yeah?'

They heard heavy footsteps on the landing above, and a younger man leaned over the banisters. He looked like an American football player – powerfully built, with shoulders like he was still wearing padding. Like his brother, his hair was dark, but cut in a more trendy style and he wore a heavy gold bracelet and an expensive looking watch on his wrist.

'What the . . .?' He came down the stairs in a rush. 'What are those kids doing here?'

'Lost. They want to use the phone. Show them where it is, will you?'

'We don't want any kids round here,' Ian snarled. His eyes were pin-points of black. 'Next thing you know they'll be swarming all over the place – snooping around, pinching bits of machinery . . .'

The older man gave a snort of laughter. 'Don't be daft, man. Girls, that's all they are. Still at school, I bet.'

He made it sound like an insult. Holly could feel her anger rising.

'We don't steal,' she said indignantly. 'And if you'll just let us use the phone, we'll be gone and you won't see us again – ever.'

'I tell you, they're bad news,' said Ian. 'Chuck 'em out.'

The older man's jaw tightened. 'I thought I told you to show them to the phone. Now, are you going to do it or not?'

'Do it yourself.' Ian strode out of the door, slamming it behind him.

'Sorry about that.' A flush of anger darkened his cheeks. 'My brother's not too happy about teenagers. We've had a lot of vandalism since we moved to Framley. My name's Clough, Thomas Clough. I'll show you where the phone is.'

Holly was still looking at the gun. Following the direction of her gaze, the man gave a thin smile. 'You're quite safe,' he said. 'I've been shooting foxes in the woods on the cliff.'

He put the gun down and showed them into a room crammed with filing cabinets, a couple of chairs and a desk overflowing with bills and bits of paper. 'Help yourself,' he said, sweeping a few papers to one side so they could reach the phone.

'Do you have a directory?' Holly asked. 'I don't know her office number.'

Thomas Clough gave her a questioning look.

'She's an estate agent,' Holly told him. 'Earnshaw's.'

He passed the directory across the desk. 'I know the one. A tough lady.'

It didn't take long to explain what had happened. She didn't tell Carole about being shot at – not with Thomas Clough standing right beside her.

'I'll come and pick you up. Wait right there.'

'We'll be outside the gate,' Holly said hastily.

'Let me speak to Mr Clough.'

Reluctantly, Holly handed him the phone. 'My aunt wants to speak to you.'

She crossed over to Belinda and Tracy by the window. There was something about the way they looked at her. A suppressed excitement that she couldn't quite understand.

Tracy tugged at her hand and gave a slight nod towards the window. What on earth were they getting at?

Holly looked out, but could see nothing startling. An overgrown garden, a pick-up truck with 'CLOUGH BROS' on the side, a rusty old piece of farm machinery and a small trailer. So what?

Thomas Clough put the phone down. 'Your aunt wants to see me about Wetherby's Farm. This way.'

At least the living-room was better than the office. The furniture was old and rather dusty, but it had a lived-in feeling, and a fire in the grate took the chill off the sunless room.

'Coffee?' he asked. 'Or would you prefer Coke?'

'Coke, please.'

He nodded and went out of the room.

'Did you see?' Tracy said, her voice low.

'See? See what?'

'On the roof of the pick-up truck.'

'I don't know what you're talking about.'

'The searchlight,' Belinda cut in impatiently. 'It was right under your nose.'

35

A searchlight! How could she have missed it? Rushing to the window she peered out. But this window faced a different way. Thank goodness the others had seen it.

When Thomas Clough returned they drank their Cokes in near silence. Tracy made one or two stabs at conversation with him. She was pretty good at that usually, but this time it didn't work, and they were relieved to hear the doorbell ring.

Holly jumped up. 'That'll be Aunt Carole.'

'Wait here. I'll bring her through.'

'Your father said I must be mad to take you three for the holidays.' Carole laughed as she came into the room. 'I'm beginning to think he was right.' She turned to Thomas Clough. 'Thank you for looking after them.'

'Not at all. Now, you wanted to talk to me about Wetherby's Farm.'

Carole was frank. 'Mrs Wetherby wants to sell her farm, but she thinks that some of the things that are happening around here are upsetting that. And she puts them down to you, Mr Clough. Do you know what she is talking about?'

'You bet I know what she's talking about. She's complained about them often enough.' His voice was harsh. 'The old bat is out of her mind. Says we roam about at night opening gates . . . stealing her animals. She's mad I tell you.'

'Calm down, Mr Clough. I know my client is elderly and may be difficult to handle but it is true that some of her sheep have strayed recently, haven't they? And only last week one of them was found floating in the sea – dead.'

'I know. I know. But that doesn't mean it's anything to do with us. And as for the bit about lights and mysterious noises . . . it's all in her imagination. She's crazy, I tell you. I'd be willing to buy the property just to get her off my back – but not at the ridiculous price she's asking.'

'How much would you be prepared to offer?'

He drew a piece of scrap paper towards him. He scribbled a few figures, thought for a minute and did a calculation. Then he crossed it out and started again. Finally, he pushed the paper towards her.

Carole looked at it coolly. 'You spoke of a ridiculous figure. This is laughable. Goodbye, Mr Clough. Come on, girls.'

'That told him,' Holly giggled as they got in the car. Thomas Clough was standing in the porch glaring after them as they drew away, his face red with anger.

'Was the offer really that low?' Belinda asked.

Carole grinned. 'Not that bad,' she said. 'On the low side, but I would guess that he might be persuaded to raise it.'

'Do you mean these things aren't really happening?' Tracy asked, admiration in her voice. 'No, that can't be right. We saw the lights, and we were shot at.'

'You were what!' Carole swivelled round in her seat.

'Careful!' Holly gasped. 'You nearly ran into the hedge.'

Carole stopped the car. 'Tell me.'

'It was when we were lost,' Holly told her. 'We saw the warning notices by the Ministry of Defence, and all of a sudden we heard a shot go whistling by. We took cover, but there wasn't another one.' Holly knew it sounded weak and a lot less frightening than it had been.

'Maybe they weren't shooting at us,' she interrupted herself. 'Maybe it was foxes. Thomas Clough said he'd been out shooting foxes. Maybe it was that.'

Carole laughed. 'Probably. I thought you were serious for a moment.'

We were, Holly thought. *How do we know he's telling the truth?*

'Funny place to have a scrapyard,' Tracy said.

'That's not it. It's in Framley. Right in the town centre.' Carole sounded thoughtful, her mind still on their earlier conversation.

'Did you say warning notices from the Ministry of Defence? As far as I know they haven't any land around here. The island, of course – but not on the mainland. Are you sure?'

'Of course we're sure. The notices were every few hundred metres. We were right on the edge of the cliff when we saw the first one. Some of the barbed-wire and posts had fallen over.'

Carole put the car into gear. 'Odd,' she said thoughtfully.

They drove out through the main gate and on to the dirt track. Carole switched on the lights and the windscreen wipers. 'I'll be glad when this mist lifts,' she said. 'It makes everything so cold and damp.'

They had just rounded the first bend when they saw lights coming towards them. Holly watched with a slight edge of nervousness. It was a big, bulky vehicle – a Land Rover or something like that – and going pretty fast for such a narrow road.

'Move over,' Carole muttered, tucking in nearer to the hedge.

But it was as if the driver didn't care. As if he hadn't seen them. If anything, the vehicle veered even further over on to their side of the road.

He'll slow down in a minute, Holly thought. At any moment she expected to hear the scream of brakes . . . see the other car swerve away. *He must stop*, she told herself. It was unbelievable to think that he wouldn't. Then, with numb certainty, she realised he wasn't going to.

'My God!' Carole said. 'He's going to hit us.'

She slammed her foot on the brakes and steered towards the hedge.

There was a sickening scrape of metal on metal as the other car nudged the front bumper and swerved away. Holly was flung forward. Then the seat-belt caught her and she jolted back against the headrest.

For a moment the car balanced on two wheels, then slowly tilted over on its side into the ditch, leaning heavily against the hedge. How many seconds she lay there, Holly had no idea. She just knew she felt sick. Her head hurt, and she couldn't stop shaking.

'Is everyone all right?'

It was Carole's voice. Holly couldn't quite make out where it was coming from. Everything was at a peculiar angle. 'Holly?'

'Yes, I'm OK. Belinda? Tracy?'

Slowly they sorted themselves out, released seat-belts and looked at one another. There was only one side they could get out, and even that was sticking up in the air. If they weren't careful, the car might tip right over.

'One at a time,' Carole said. 'And very gradually. No quick movements, please. You first, Holly.'

Holly pressed the lever and tried to open the door but it was jammed.

'What's that smell?' Belinda said suddenly.

'Petrol.'

Carole's terse reply gave Holly added strength, and she managed to force the door open. Wriggling out, she dropped to the ground and opened the back door to help Tracy out. From there on it was fairly easy. One by one they inched their way out of the car until at last they were all standing on the grass verge.

Carole checked the fuel tank. 'No damage done, thank heavens. I didn't fancy being roasted alive.'

'Nor me.' They grinned at one another, relieved that the danger was over.

It was only after they had finally managed to get the car upright and back on the road that they realised the other car had driven on without stopping.

Carole shook her head in disbelief. 'He could have killed us. Did anyone get the number? I'm not even sure what make it was. Does anyone know?'

'Sorry. I just couldn't believe he was going to do it,' Tracy said.

'Nor me. He deliberately pushed us into the ditch,' Belinda said indignantly. 'All I know is, it was cream or white.'

Carole nodded. 'That's the impression I got too. At least the damage doesn't look too serious. The bodywork's in a bit of a mess, but as long as the engine's OK . . . Let's go.'

The car spluttered and coughed a bit when it first started, but after spitting out a plug of grass from the back end it was OK. Carole reported the accident at the police station on the way back, but the police weren't very hopeful about catching him.

'It's the holiday season you see, Miss. They come from all around. If you didn't see the number . . .' His sentence hung in the air. He obviously didn't think much of their detective powers.

'It's time we wrote all this down,' Holly said after dinner that evening. 'It didn't seem worth it at first. But now I think there's much more to it.' She put the red Mystery Club notebook down on the coffee table, and turned to a fresh page.

'Oh, no,' Belinda groaned. 'I didn't know you'd brought that. You told your father you weren't going to get involved in anything while we were here. You said it was just a holiday.'

'And it is. But I brought the notebook just in case. When I was editing the paper for my school at Highgate – before we moved to Willow Vale – I learned never to go anywhere without a notebook. Maybe I can write this up for our school magazine.'

'Steffie will be mad if you do,' Tracy grinned. 'She's scared stiff that you're after her job. She's probably planned her editorial already.'

'*And* arranged the rest of the news stories,' Belinda said. 'How can she make them so boring? You'd make a much better editor, Holly.'

'Maybe,' Holly said glumly, 'but there's not much chance of that while Steffie's around. Anyway, let's get on with the Mystery Club book. We'll start with the lights. They came from the island first. Green and white and red. Then from this side there were several greens and a white. I didn't see any red. Did you?'

'But in the afternoon I didn't see any green,' Tracy objected.

'Yes, I'll put that down,' Holly said. 'It might be important. What's the next bit?'

'Don't forget the searchlight on the truck,' Belinda reminded her.

'The car pushing us off the road is the big thing,' Tracy said.

'The police didn't believe us when we said it was deliberate,' Belinda said, "just someone fooling around," they said. But it wasn't, was it?'

Holly shook her head, writing furiously. 'No. It was definitely deliberate. But why? And more important – who?'

Tracy frowned. 'It could be that Ian guy.'

'He didn't want us around the Grange, that's for sure. I don't believe all that stuff about vandalism. I wonder who the pick-up truck with the searchlight belongs to? And what was Thomas really doing with the gun?' Belinda asked.

'I think we need to find out a lot more about the Clough brothers and their scrap business, don't you?' Holly's eyes sparkled. There was nothing she liked better than to ferret out information – especially if it involved a bit of danger. 'I know what Miss Marple would do . . .' She closed the red notebook firmly.

'I can guess,' Belinda muttered. 'Another long walk in the rain.'

'We're going into Framley,' Holly said, 'We're taking our swimsuits and towels – just as anyone would when they're on holiday. And we'll wander round the town and look at the shops. And if we just happen to come across a scrapyard, well, it would be perfectly natural for us to have a look round, wouldn't it?'

She put on an innocent look, but the smile that curved the corners of her mouth was decidedly wicked. 'You never know what you might find . . .' she said.

4 The killing island

Sun poured through the curtains, painting the walls with stripes of yellow. Holly could smell fresh coffee and toast.

'Breakfast!' Carole's voice floated up the stairs.

Holly threw back the duvet and grabbed her bathrobe. 'Come on, you two,' she called. 'It's a gorgeous day and we've lots to do.' She hurried down to the kitchen, followed in a few minutes by Belinda.

'Where's Tracy?'

Carole looked up from a letter she was reading. 'You're miles too late for your energetic friend. She was up an hour ago. Gone for a run along the beach.'

Five minutes later Tracy arrived, her short blonde hair tousled, her cheeks glowing.

'What a fantastic day,' she gasped. 'I've been all the way to Framley and back. I'm starving.'

'Help yourself.' Carole pushed the jug of orange juice and cereal packets towards her, then put two more slices of bread in the toaster.

Tracy poured herself a bowl of muesli and gulped down a glass of juice. 'Guess what I saw,' she said as Carole went out of the room.

'What?'

'A white Land Rover with a damaged front wing on the driver's side.'

'You didn't!' Holly was so excited she almost poured the milk into the marmalade. 'Did you get the number?'

Tracy shook her head. 'Wrong angle. I was down on the beach. He was in a line of traffic on the Esplanade. I couldn't even see the driver clearly – except that he had dark hair.'

Holly's face lit up. 'So does Ian Clough. And Thomas.'

'So do half the population of Framley, I should think,' Belinda said dryly.

Carole came back into the room dressed in a business suit. 'I'm dropping my car off to be repaired on my way to work. It will probably take a while, so if you want to be mobile for the next few days I suggest you hire bikes. There's a shop in Framley – near the harbour. And, Holly . . .'

Holly looked up enquiringly.

'A quiet, incident-free day, eh? No getting shot at. No tangles with the Ministry of Defence or the Clough brothers? Just a plain, ordinary day. Promise?'

'Sure. We were going into Framley anyway. We

thought we'd explore, have a look at the harbour. Go swimming perhaps. But it's a great idea about the bikes. We'll do that.'

'Good. See you this evening.'

They walked into Framley, the sun hot on their backs in spite of a stiff breeze. There was a café facing the harbour and Belinda suggested they go in for an ice cream to cool off.

Sitting in the window, they had a good view of all that was going on. Holly noticed a trim white yacht lying at anchor with a girl sunbathing on deck. A boy came out of one of the cabins to speak to her and the girl pulled on a T-shirt and shorts and they both came ashore.

Tracy's eyes followed them. 'Fantastic to be on a yacht in this weather.'

'I'm not into boats,' Belinda said. 'Dad's always trying to get me interested. We had our own yacht for a bit, but I'd rather ride Meltdown any day.'

'We *had* noticed,' Holly grinned.

The door clanged, and the couple from the yacht came in.

The boy was older than he'd looked from a distance. Seventeen, perhaps – or even eighteen. He was tall with long legs and an athletic body. 'What do you fancy, Tiffany?' he asked the girl.

She was shorter than him, but Holly could see at once that they were brother and sister. They had the same wide mouth, the same brown eyes, and the same easy manner. The girl glanced at the menu on the counter. 'A Rocky Horror. I'll try that.'

'Greedy pig. I'm having a coffee.'

The girl sauntered past them to the next table. 'Hi,' she said briefly, almost without looking at them.

The boy followed her a few minutes later, a coffee in one hand and a tall glass piled high with ice cream and chocolate sauce in the other. His eyes brightened when he saw the three girls, and his greeting was considerably warmer than his sister's.

'Mind if we join you?' he asked.

They introduced themselves as Paul and Tiffany Middleton. 'Was it you I saw going for a run on the beach earlier on?' he asked.

Tracy nodded.

'I thought so. Not many people go jogging around here.'

'What are you doing in Framley?' Holly asked.

'Mum and Dad are looking for a place to build an inn,' he said. 'We thought we'd found it, but the estate agent said there was a danger of anthrax spores spreading over from the island.'

He jerked his head towards the approximate direction of the Bight.

Holly's spine tingled. 'Are you talking about Wetherby's Farm?'

Paul shrugged. 'I can't remember the name. We saw the details in the estate agent in the town. It needs a lot of work done on it but it has plenty of space, and the price was right. Mum and Dad were quite keen till the guy told us about the anthrax. He said several dogs had become ill after visiting the Bight and one of the farm's sheep had died mysteriously a few days ago.'

'I'd never heard of anthrax,' Tiffany said. 'But it sounds horrific. Mr Hare said the island could be lethal for ever. It's a bit too close to the mainland for my liking.'

'That sheep died mysteriously all right,' Holly said angrily. 'It fell down the cliff because someone opened the farm gates.'

'You've only Mrs Wetherby's word for that,' Tracy warned. 'She might be as batty as people say she is.'

'The island can't be as dangerous as all that,' maintained Holly. 'Someone's there, or how would we see those lights? So why is the estate agent warning people off? Doesn't he want to sell it?'

There was no answer to that, but Holly was determined that one way or the other she was going to find out what was going on.

The others were still talking, but it was nearly lunch-time. There was no time to waste. 'Sorry, we've got to go,' she said. 'Have you seen a scrapyard around here anywhere?'

Paul looked puzzled. 'A scrapyard? What for?'

She couldn't think of any good reason why they should want to find a scrapyard, and there was no way she was going to tell Paul about the Mystery Club. 'I'm looking for a second-hand bike,' she improvised. Well, that was more or less true anyway.

As they got up to pay the bill, Holly noticed a man at the next table. He got up and followed them up to the counter – leaving his meal half finished.

They were almost at the corner of the road when the man caught up with them. He was dark, powerfully built, wearing a navy blue jersey and coarse black trousers. His accent was Spanish, though he spoke good English.

'I heard what you say. You want the scrapyard?' he asked. 'I work there sometimes. Follow me.'

'Er . . . no thanks,' said Holly. 'We don't want to take you out of your way.'

'No trouble. This way.'

With uneasy glances at one another, the girls followed him down a side street.

The gates to the scrapyard were closed and the board said,

CLOUGH BROS. SCRAP DEALERS. KEEP OUT.

'Thank you,' Holly said. 'Do you know when it opens again?'

'Soon,' he said. 'Adios.' And he hurried away.

'Strange guy,' Tracy said. 'How long is soon?'

Belinda frowned. 'And how do they expect to get customers if they tell them to keep out?'

'You can't see the board when the gates are open, silly,' Holly said with a laugh.

The heavy double gates were padlocked and there was no way anyone could see through the corrugated iron fence, but there was a small door in the left-hand gate – just big enough to squeeze through.

Holly turned the handle. It was unlocked. 'Here we go then,' she said. 'This will do nicely.'

Belinda hung back. 'Do you think we ought to?'

'No. But we're going to anyway.' Holly gave a push and the door swung noisily open.

They ducked through and stood at the entrance, dwarfed by towering avenues of junk and rusting machinery. Tracy whistled in amazement.

Holly looked around. 'OK. So we're in. That's a start anyway.'

'What are we looking for?' Tracy asked. 'Not a second-hand bike, I guess?'

Holly ticked them off on her fingers. 'One, the white Land Rover that you saw this morning. Two, the pick-up truck with a searchlight on the roof, and three, a clue as to why someone is signalling the island.'

Belinda frowned. 'What kind of a clue?'

'I don't know yet. But we'll know it when we see it. Tracy, you take the middle aisle. Belinda, you take the left one, and I'll do the right. See you at the far end.'

'What do we say if someone comes?' Belinda asked.

'Tell them we're looking for a second-hand bike?' Tracy suggested.

Holly giggled. 'That'll do nicely.'

Although it was the middle of the day and the sun was shining, there was a stiff breeze and it was quite spooky walking alone between towering piles of scrap. Everything seemed to have a life of its own, creaking and groaning in the wind.

Holly caught sight of a billowing tarpaulin covering a large object. A tyre peeked out below the canvas. Was it a car? Her pulse quickened and she yanked at the heavy green tarpaulin.

With loud squeaking and a flurry of movement, a family of rats skittered away. Holly screamed and let go of the tarpaulin, but the movement set the pile of metal moving and a bundle of steel bed-irons plunged to the ground at her feet. She gulped. Another foot and it would have come crashing down on her.

She heard thudding feet, and Tracy skidded up

the aisle towards her, followed a moment later by Belinda.

Behind her glasses, Belinda's eyes were wide with fear. 'What's the matter? What did you see?'

Holly's heart gradually returned to its normal beat. 'It's OK,' she said. 'Sorry if I scared you. Only rats, that's all.'

Belinda shuddered. 'Only?'

'If you're hoping for an action replay,' Tracy drawled, 'I can tell you you've got no chance. I just about broke my own record on that run. No more screams, right?'

'Right.' Although Tracy was only joking, Holly knew they'd better be careful. If she'd been that bit nearer . . . Her mind slid away from the thought of what could have happened. And to her disappointment, the hidden object turned out to be nothing more than a pile of old tyres.

Belinda and Tracy padded back to their own aisles and Holly continued down the line, being more careful poking and prodding among the half hidden pieces.

At the far end they met up. There was no need to ask if they had found anything. Their disappointed faces told her all she needed to know.

'Now what?' Tracy said with a sigh.

'Let's go and get those bikes,' Belinda pleaded. 'This place is creepy.'

'Hang on a minute,' Holly said. 'There's a

Portakabin over there. If it's the office we might find something that will give us a clue what's going on. Come on.'

The Portakabin was unlocked too. 'Considering that guy told us there'd been a lot of vandalism since they moved to Framley, they're very trusting. You'd think he'd lock the office, wouldn't you?'

'I'm not going in there,' Belinda said firmly. 'I'll keep watch.'

Tracy laughed. 'You couldn't spot a lion if it came roaring towards you. We'll both wait here and leave Holly to do the detective bit. You look that way, I'll look this.' They stationed themselves at either side of the building and Holly went inside.

It was like the room Thomas Clough used as an office at Framley Grange, only even more untidy and very much dirtier. The walls were hung with maps, adverts, and notices – most of them dusty and curling with age. One map caught Holly's attention immediately.

It was a large scale view of the coastal area from Framley to the Bight and showed the island in every detail. Alongside it was a yellowing photocopy of a newspaper cutting. Holly moved up closer to read the article:

'Anthrax Island', as it is commonly called, is an outcrop

of rock, three hundred feet high in parts and lying off Fram Bight.

It is one and a half miles long and a mile wide. At one time the island supported eleven families, but today it is inhabited solely by colonies of seabirds which nest on its craggy shoreline. Their cries are the only sounds to break the silence of this sad, abandoned place.

During the Second World War, a series of secret experiments were conducted here in order to produce an anthrax bomb. These were eventually produced and tested on the island's sheep population. Whether the bombs were actually used on the enemy is not known. Details are strictly classified and no one is allowed to live, or even land, on the island.

Anthrax is highly infectious and a killer. It occurs naturally in sheep and cattle but is equally lethal in man. Whether handled – through contaminated meat – or inhaled, the tiniest of doses produces symptoms within hours and death follows soon after in ninety per cent of the cases.

Anthrax Island is not expected to be decontaminated for many years and may never return to civil ownership.

There was a picture of the island, and across it, scrawled in pencil, was a date almost fifteen years earlier. Holly stared at it thoughtfully. Not expected to be decontaminated for many years? But how many years? Someone was there now, so whoever it was must think it was safe.

If eleven families had once lived there, then somewhere on the island there must be cottages – or at least their ruins. What if that someone was living in one of those cottages?

Holly turned her attention to the map. There in a valley were the unmistakeable signs of a road, a jetty, and a small village.

Holly looked at the mainland. No wonder no one in Framley had seen the lights. From that angle they would have been completely shielded.

'Found anything?' Tracy called.

'You bet.'

Closing the Portakabin door behind her, Holly told Tracy and Belinda what she had found. 'It says that Anthrax Island won't be decontaminated for many years. But it doesn't say exactly when. And it was written ages ago. It may have already happened. Someone is there now – that's for sure. And the only way that person can communicate with the mainland is by signalling with lights.'

Tracy looked puzzled. 'What's wrong with a phone?'

'Use your head,' Belinda said. 'How could you apply for a telephone line from an island that's supposed to be uninhabited?'

'What about a mobile phone?'

'No good,' Belinda said firmly. 'The signal wouldn't be strong enough.'

'OK then,' Holly said. 'What might they want to use the island for?'

'Maybe they're terrorists,' Tracy said. 'Maybe there are still some anthrax bombs on the island

and they're planning to bring them over to blow up the Houses of Parliament . . .'

'Anthrax wouldn't produce that kind of bomb,' Belinda said. 'They don't blow up buildings. It's germ warfare. They make people and animals sick. So sick that they die.'

Holly's eyes suddenly brightened. 'Drugs,' she said. 'Why couldn't they be bringing in drugs?'

Tracy frowned. 'But why dump them on the island first? Why not bring them straight on to the mainland?'

'You've got a point there,' Holly admitted. 'Let's go and get those bikes. We can talk about it on the way home.'

Still talking, they began to walk up the middle aisle. They hardly noticed the sound of an engine's purr until it suddenly swelled into a deep-throated roar.

Startled, they halted in their tracks. 'What the – ?'

But Holly didn't get to finish her sentence. A huge yellow crane was lumbering up the aisle, and suspended above them in the claws of the jib hung a battered old car.

'Look out!' Tracy yelled as the jib began to swing towards them.

5 Run for your life

'Run!'

Without waiting to see if the others were following, Tracy started skimming up the aisle away from the crane. With a wail Belinda started after her. Holly grabbed her hand and pulled her along. Belinda was fantastic with horses, but she was no runner – that was for sure.

Tracy was at the gates in seconds, but the inner door through which they had entered was now firmly locked. She tugged wildly, and the others soon joined in. They threw themselves at it, kicking and banging with their fists. But the lock was strong, the wood solid. There was no way to break out.

The machine was almost upon them, the jib swinging above their heads. They couldn't stay where they were. As one, they turned and ran towards the office they had just left. Heavily the crane rounded the corner and continued its relentless chase.

Holly's mind was working furiously. 'No good

staying together,' she gasped. 'We'll have to split up. When we get to the office, peel off. Take the aisles you went down when we first got here. He can't chase us all. He'll have to choose.'

'I bet he'll pick me,' Belinda wailed.

'I'll try to head him off,' Tracy said. 'I'm the fastest.'

In front of the office they stopped for a moment to get their breath back as the huge machine swung towards them. 'Go for it!' Tracy yelled, giving Belinda a push, but before she could move they heard a whine of gears and the giant claws opened, dropping their load.

With a mind-shattering explosion of sound the battered car hit the ground, just missing them. That was enough. As if a starter pistol had gone off, the girls raced away.

The car bounced sideways, sending up a cloud of dust. Then the jib dropped down – the claws open to grab another load of junk. Greedily the claws closed and once more swung aloft.

Holly, crouched beneath an overhanging ledge of metal, saw the cabin of the crane swing round and the machine lumber away up the main aisle. If only she could see the driver, she thought. But the cabin was too high, the driver's face hidden behind the glass.

Seizing her chance, she slipped into the Portakabin and picked up the phone to ring the emergency services. No. By the time she explained and got someone to believe her, it would be too late. They had to get out of this themselves.

Crouching down behind the desk so that she couldn't be seen, Holly glanced through the back window. There were two packing cases propped against the fence. They were big, but not enormous, with a strange curved logo of a red knot on green. If they weren't too heavy perhaps she could get one on top of the other. Then they could climb up and get over the wall.

She slipped out of the back door and struggled to balance one of the cases at an angle, so that she could take the weight on her back. Then, she edged it against the other case and with a terrible effort managed to tip it on top.

Don't fall, she commanded them.

Tracy and Belinda were at the far end, the crane blocking their exit. Holly willed them to run in opposite directions. 'This way,' she signalled.

Belinda stumbled past the machine and headed for the office. Grabbing a big spanner that was lying on a shelf, Holly flung open the door. 'Behind the shed!' she yelled. 'Climb over the wall.'

Then she raced up behind the crane and threw the spanner as hard as she could. The sound of breaking glass distracted the driver momentarily.

'Tracy! This way,' Holly shouted. 'Quick.'

They both reached the packing cases at the

same time, and climbed up. The cases swayed ominously, and as Holly scrambled over the wall, she heard a tremendous crash.

Good, she said to herself. That would stop them being followed – at least for a few minutes.

They dropped into a muddy lane on the other side and lay there for a moment, winded.

Belinda was fumbling round in the gutter. 'I've lost my glasses.'

Holly sat up, groaning. 'None of the detectives in the books I've read ever has this trouble. Why does it have to happen to me? Couldn't you wear contact lenses or something?'

'I don't like them,' Belinda said.

'OK,' Tracy said. 'Don't move. You'll probably step on them. We'll find them.'

While Tracy was looking for Belinda's spectacles, Holly examined their surroundings. 'We wasted a lot of effort for nothing,' she said. 'There's a door here. It must have been behind the packing cases.'

It was a small wooden door, surprisingly sturdy considering the state of the junkyard. Holly turned the handle and leaned against it to see if it would open, but it was locked solid.

Tracy got up off her knees, Belinda's glasses in her hand. She wiped the lenses on the sleeve of her T-shirt and handed them back. 'Next time you try leaping over a two-metre wall take your glasses off first!'

'Next time I see a two-metre wall, I'll keep well away from you two,' Belinda retorted.

'I wonder what happened to the crane driver,' Holly said as they made their way along the lane. 'I wish I knew which one he was. It's bound to be one of the brothers.'

'Or the Spanish guy,' Belinda said. 'I noticed him in the café. He was listening to everything we said. He knew we were on to something, and he was the only one who knew where we were.'

Tracy gave a satisfied smile. 'Whoever it was won't be happy about that smashed window. That was a fantastic shot.'

Holly glanced nervously around. 'Come on, we'd better get going before someone comes looking for us. We're asking to get caught standing here.'

'I'm starving,' Belinda grumbled.

Holly glanced at her watch. 'Me too. Let's find the place that hires out bikes. Then we'll go home and get something to eat.'

They were back at Aunt Carole's and eating lunch in less than an hour. As they stacked the plates into the dishwasher, Tracy spotted a pair of binoculars hanging in their case behind the kitchen door.

'These might come in handy,' she said. 'When we were in the States Dad always took binoculars with him when he went on a hunting trip.' She took the binoculars out of their case and looked through them. 'Wow. Fantastic magnification. Much better than my dad's.' She examined them critically. 'Carole won't mind if we borrow them, will she?'

Holly shrugged uneasily. Her mother was pretty fussy about taking things without asking. Maybe Aunt Carole would be too. After all, they were sisters. But what would be the harm in borrowing them as long as they were careful?

She took the case from Tracy. 'I expect it will be OK.'

They were on the road again by three o'clock, this time heading for the Bight instead of Framley town. Cycling was better than the car or walking, Holly decided. The breeze had dropped and this time they didn't go over the Common, but stuck to the winding track that ran between fields of heather and bracken.

About a quarter of a mile beyond the gates of Framley Grange they passed a woman driving a herd of cows. She was small, with grey hair tucked under a man's peaked cap. Edging past, Holly took a good look at her. The woman was thin, but she looked tough, and quite able to take care of herself.

As they passed, they heard her swear at one of the animals and tap it smartly on its rear. Holly smiled to herself. This woman wouldn't take any nonsense from anyone.

'Do you think that was Mrs Wetherby?' she

asked, after they had passed. 'She wasn't exactly the kind of person I'd been expecting.'

'I thought Mrs Wetherby would be a frail old lady with a pile of knitting,' Belinda said.

Tracy chuckled. 'This one would be more at home chopping logs. No wonder Thomas Clough was fed up. I bet she'd be quite a handful. No chance of bullying her.'

Holly grinned at the thought. 'Maybe we should have a talk with her sometime. But first let's find out where the lights are coming from.'

Beyond the farm the road disappeared altogether at the entrance to a bay so small it was hardly a bay at all. There were a couple of low sand-dunes fringed with marram grass, and a narrow stretch of rocky beach rising to cliffs at either side. On the southern side were the remains of a jetty, but the tide was so far out that it ended well out of reach of any water. Holly remembered what her aunt had told her. This must belong to the farm.

From here, the island looked amazingly close, its cliffs rising steeply out of the sea.

'We need to be higher up,' Holly said. 'Let's leave the bikes here and see how much we can see from the top.'

Chaining the bikes together, the girls walked up through the bracken to where the cliffs jutted out into the water. Holly took out the binoculars. They were now above the level of the island and she could see flat land with a pattern of what had once been fields, and a road dotted with the remains of cottages.

'No sign of life there,' she said.

But Tracy was looking elsewhere. 'Have you noticed?' she said. 'We're inside that barbed-wire fence with the notices about the Ministry of Defence.'

Holly looked puzzled. 'Weird. There was no warning when we walked up from the road.'

She walked to the edge of the cliff and looked down. 'There's a cove a bit further along. It looks as if we could get down to it fairly easily. Now we're here we might as well explore.'

'You two go,' Belinda said. 'I'll stay here.'

'Not that you're too lazy to go,' Tracy said dryly. 'It's just for our protection, isn't it? So you can keep an eye on us.'

'You bet,' Belinda agreed with a smile. 'I'm dying to go rock climbing really, but I'll make the sacrifice and stay behind.'

Holly gave her a playful shove. 'I'll leave the binoculars with you in case I drop them on the rocks.'

Belinda sat down while Holly and Tracy made for the cove.

The descent was more dangerous than it looked. A path wound round in a series of hairpin bends, crossing and criss-crossing a deep crevice which gradually grew wider and wider. The pathway finally ducked beneath an arch of rock and disappeared into a tunnel.

Tracy skidded to a standstill, sending a small avalanche of shale rattling down the rocks. Holly cannoned into her and sat down abruptly. 'Ow! What did you do that for?' She picked herself up, her hands pitted with sharp stones.

'Listen. I can hear the sea swishing about. What if we get sucked into deep water inside the tunnel?'

Holly listened. She could hear water, but it sounded a long way away. Still, they'd have to be careful. The tide was out. If it came in fast they might get trapped. 'We'll take it slowly, and hang on to the rocks as we go.'

They ducked under the arch and down a broad slope into darkness. Holly wished she had thought to bring a torch, but it was too late now. The glimmer of light ahead did nothing to lighten this part of the tunnel.

Water dripped from the roof with a steady *plop!* . . . *plop!* They felt their way, sliding their hands along a slimy rock face. Underfoot it had now levelled off, but Holly and Tracy had stumbled into so many pools in those first few minutes that their trainers were soaked.

Gradually, their eyes became accustomed to the gloom. Holly could see that they were in a cave, the floor of which had been roughly concreted. Someone had been here before them. There had been a tunnel off to the right at one time, but it had been boarded up. A very professional-looking job too.

'I wonder what they used this for?' Tracy said. 'Do you think it might have been the Ministry of Defence? During the Second World War, I mean? Like the island. Maybe that's what all the notices were about. To stop people finding out about this.'

'It could be,' Holly said slowly. 'But Carole didn't think the Ministry had any land around here – except the island. I wonder . . .'

She felt all round the edges of the board. It was smooth and dry. Not the way you would expect it to feel if it had stood there untouched for years. She knelt down on the damp concrete and tried to wriggle her fingers underneath.

'Hey, Tracy. Your fingers are thinner than mine. Can you feel anything?'

Tracy knelt down beside her, probing the space behind the board. 'There's something . . . feels like a cable for an electric kettle . . . No, it's thicker than that.'

Holly managed to hold her excitement in check. 'Could it be for a signalling lamp?' she asked. 'Like the lights we saw from Belinda's room?'

Tracy looked up, her eyes shining. 'You bet it could. But what do they use for electricity?'

'Maybe they could run it off a car battery. Maybe

they've got their own generator in there. Anyway, let's get out in the fresh air.'

They inched their way forward and up a steep slope until they were once more in daylight – in the cove they had seen from the top of the cliffs. And it was a relief to be breathing in salt spray after the stale air in the tunnel.

The sea had already covered the rocks on either side of the cove so that they were completely cut off. But Holly was certain that if they'd got down OK, they could easily manage to get back.

Holly and Tracy sat together on a flat rock, trying to take in the meaning of what they had seen. The lights *must* be coming from here. They were clearly some kind of signal. But for what?

The swish of the sea was soothing, and it took a few minutes for the waspish note of a powerboat engine to bring them back to reality.

'What are you two doing here?' A man's voice startled Holly.

There were two men in the boat – both dressed completely in white. White rubberised suits with hoods, high rubber boots and thick white gloves.

They looked like something out of a science fiction movie. The man who had shouted at them looked vaguely familiar, but it wasn't either of the two Clough brothers. Perhaps it was someone they'd seen in the harbour, Holly thought. It would be hard to recognise anyone in that gear.

The other man was thickset and ugly with a scar down one cheek.

'Just looking around,' Holly said. 'We're not doing any harm.'

'Clear off! This place is forbidden. It's Ministry of Defence property. The whole area is contaminated by biological pollution. You want to die?'

Tracy stared at him defiantly. 'There's no need to be rude. And we're not deaf either.'

'Cheeky devils,' the other man snarled. 'I'll fix them. I'll fix them good.'

'Cool it, Frank. They're going.'

'I'll say they're going.' The scar was a purple stripe down his pale face.

The other man was calmer. 'This cove is poisoned with anthrax germs. Why do you suppose we're wearing these protective uniforms? Stay away from here. And that's an order.'

'Tell them to keep their mouths shut, if they want to stay alive,' Scarface growled.

The other man turned on him sharply. 'Shut it, Frank.'

The threat from Scarface was too real to be ignored. He wasn't joking. Tracy and Holly turned and went back into the cave without looking back.

'They're not from the Ministry of Defence,' Holly muttered.

'More like from the Ministry of Thugs.'

They could still hear the powerboat's engine. A shivery feeling in Holly's spine told her that Scarface was only waiting for an excuse to come after them.

They didn't stop until they were back on the cliff top, but there was no sign of anyone. Then a clump of bracken stirred, and Belinda's anxious face looked out.

'What are you doing there?' Tracy laughed.

'I was hiding.'

'Why?' Tracy looked puzzled.

'You know when you were walking down that zigzag path? I was watching a couple of nesting seabirds with the binoculars, and I happened to focus on the island. There was a man there, watching you through a high-powered telescope. He flashed a signal to the other side of the island and suddenly a boat appeared from what looked like a sheer rock face. Honestly, it was a real mystery where it came from . . . it came out of nowhere.'

'How come the man didn't see you?' Holly asked anxiously.

'I ducked down in the bracken as soon as I spotted him.'

'And?'

'This powerboat appeared like magic, heading straight for the cove. It was going like crazy. After a while it went zooming back to the island and

70

disappeared again. I thought they'd murdered you or something.'

'I thought you were staying up here to protect us,' Tracy said with a grin.

Belinda flushed. 'I'd have gone to the police if you hadn't turned up soon.'

Tracy turned to scan the horizon. 'Great. We'd have been dead by then.'

Belinda shrugged. 'Sorry.'

'Did you know about the forbidden cove at the Bight?' Holly asked her aunt over supper.

'A forbidden cove?' Carole looked puzzled. 'I haven't heard of one. What do you mean?'

Tracy helped herself to more salad. 'We found this cove,' she said. 'A couple of men in a boat shouted at us to keep away. They said it was dangerous.'

'That's strange,' Carole said thoughtfully. 'I don't know anything about such a place.'

Belinda took up the story. 'I was watching from the cliff top. I saw this boat come zooming out from the island, and – *ow*!'

'Sorry,' Holly said sweetly. 'Did I kick you?'

Belinda scowled and rubbed her ankle.

Holly changed her line of enquiry. 'Who would I go to if I wanted to know when the island would be cleared of anthrax?'

'I've no idea,' said Carole. 'The coastguards perhaps. What made you think of that?'

Holly shrugged. 'Nothing really.' She was saved from further questioning by the telephone. 'Shall I go?' she asked.

'Yes. If it's for me, tell them I'm out. I'll ring them back tomorrow.

Holly picked up the phone. 'Framley 3241.'

She could hear people talking, and the sound of a juke-box. Then a man's voice said, 'Tell that aunt of yours that if you don't keep your nose out of my business, you'll all be going home in wooden boxes.'

6 Mystery watcher

'For me?' Carole asked, as Holly came back into the room.

Holly shook her head. 'No. For me.'

Her aunt studied her for a minute. 'You look pale. Anything wrong?'

'Not a thing,' Holly replied evenly.

It was evening before she had a chance to talk to Tracy and Belinda about it. 'Someone definitely thinks we're on to something. And they think we're getting too close for comfort.' Holly laughed. 'The thing is, we can't be sure what it is we're getting close to.'

'Did you recognise the voice?' Belinda asked. 'Was it the Spaniard?'

'Not a chance. No accent.'

'What about Scarface?' Tracy looked worried.

'Could be. But I can't be sure. There was so much noise going on in the background. It sounded like a pub.'

'I think we ought to tell the police,' Belinda said.

Holly shook her head. 'You know what they were like about the car. And we had concrete evidence there – with a bashed-in car to prove it.'

'And an adult witness,' Tracy broke in.

'Let's wait till we've got something to tell them that they *have* to believe,' Holly said.

Belinda chewed at her lip. 'I hope you're right,' she said at last.

That night they took it in turns to watch for the lights, and by the morning all three of them were bleary-eyed and depressed. Belinda had the last watch, but when Holly came into her room she was fast asleep.

'Wake up.' Holly shook her. 'You're not much of a watcher, are you?'

Belinda yawned. 'I stayed awake until it was light. They're not going to be signalling now. They've had all night to do it.'

That was true. The last time they'd seen the lights had been just after it got dark. 'I think it's got something to do with the tide,' Belinda said. 'It's always at high tide.'

'Belinda! You're magic,' Holly beamed. Of course. It stood to reason that high tide would be the best time for a boat to come over from the island. That way they could get right into the cove, unload and take it out at the other end of the tunnel without anyone suspecting a thing. The lights from the island would signal when they'd got the stuff and the reply from the mainland would tell them whether the coast was clear. Brilliant!

Over breakfast the Mystery Club discussed the cargo coming over from the island. 'It's got to be something illegal,' Holly said. 'And it's got to be a nice little earner for someone.'

'We've been through this before,' Tracy said. 'We said it was most likely to be explosives or drugs.'

'I've had another think,' Holly said slowly. 'If it was terrorists, surely they would land closer to a big city. How would they transport the explosives? Put it on a train marked, "BOMBS – HANDLE WITH CARE"?'

Tracy giggled. 'You've got a point there.'

Belinda swallowed a mouthful of cereal. 'It could be illegal immigrants.'

Tracy and Holly looked at her in amazement. 'You're real sharp this morning. What are you eating? Brain Flakes?'

Belinda went red. 'Well, it's obvious. You see it on the news all the time.'

So that was another thing to think about. 'I think a visit to the coastguards is called for,' Holly said.

'Oh, no,' Belinda groaned. 'Not more chasing around. I thought we were meeting Tiffany and Paul this morning.'

'We are. We're just clearing up an important point first, that's all.'

'Well, I'm going for a run first,' Tracy declared. 'I was too tired to make it earlier on. I hate missing my run. It messes up the whole day. You two go on. I'll see you in the café.'

Holly was ready first. While she was waiting she wrote up a few more details in the Mystery Club notebook, then went into Belinda's room and stood with her elbows on the window-sill. She picked up the binoculars.

The sea was as calm as if it were painted on canvas, and a yacht was lying at anchor a little way off the island. She focused on the name: *Van Dijk*.

It all looked so peaceful. It was hard to imagine that this small island had once been used for such a deadly purpose.

Holly shuddered. Someone was living over there. Or at least, was visiting the island on a regular basis. So it had to be clear. No one would chance it otherwise. Or would they?

'Those men in the powerboat,' she said slowly. 'They were dressed up like scientists – though I don't think they were from the Ministry of Defence. I suppose they couldn't *still* be making anthrax bombs over there? Only for terrorists this time?'

'Could be, but from what you told about the one with a scar he'd find it hard to add up, let alone be able to work out chemical formulas.'

Holly swallowed hard. She hoped Belinda was

right. But why else would the men be dressed in protective clothing? What did they have to hide?

When Belinda was ready they got the bikes out of the garage and cycled down to Framley Harbour.

The coastguards' office was at the harbour entrance, the last building before the lighthouse. To get to it they had to pass the wholesale fish market where the catch was sold each morning and a tiny little church, squashed between the two of them.

The buying and selling had long been over, but the smell of fish was still strong and people were busy clearing and cleaning up ready for the next day.

'Do you want to wait here or in the café?' Holly asked. 'There's no point in us both going to see the coastguard.'

'I'll go on to the café,' Belinda said happily.

They chained the bikes to a lamppost on the other side of the pavement, and Holly walked up the steps to the coastguards' office.

Belinda walked a few steps towards the café then changed her mind. The others might not have arrived yet, and she hated sitting on her own. She turned.

'Holly!' she called. 'I'll stay here.'

There was a wrought-iron bench facing the fish market, and she sat down to wait. At first, she barely noticed the group of fishermen clustered round the counter at the back of the market, but gradually she began to feel slightly uneasy.

One of the men appeared to be reading a newspaper, yet his eyes kept staring at her over the top of the page. She tried looking the other way – towards the boats rather than towards the town – but it was no good. She could feel his eyes boring in to her. She was relieved when she saw Holly come back down the steps and cross the road towards her.

'Thank goodness you're back,' she said. 'That man over there doesn't half stare.'

'What man?'

There was no sign of him now. Just a discarded newspaper in the spot where he had been.

'There *was* someone,' Belinda insisted.

'Did you recognise him?'

Belinda sighed. 'It could be the Spaniard. If so, he's had a haircut since we last saw him. But I couldn't see his face properly. It was hidden behind the paper.'

They left their bikes where they were, and walked across to the café. None of the others had arrived yet. It was just as well Belinda had waited on the bench. They took a table by the window.

Holly was bubbling with excitement. 'Guess what? The island is officially safe.' She got out the Mystery Club notebook and flipped over a couple of pages. '"Returned to civil ownership after decontamination", it says. I knew it was! I just knew!'

Belinda sipped her Coke slowly, trying to take it in. 'Then why doesn't everyone know?'

'I'm coming to that. The man who owned it when the Ministry of Defence took over is dead, and it now belongs to his son. He's pretty ancient too, I gather. Anyway, there's going to be a public announcement at the end of the month.'

'What about the notices on the cliff top?'

'I didn't actually tell anyone there were warning notices there. I just asked about MOD property on the mainland. The coastguard said there wasn't any around here. I think they're fakes.'

Belinda looked worried. 'Don't you think we ought to go to the police now?'

'Soon. When we've got more evidence to give them.'

Holly changed the subject. 'Look at that yacht coming into harbour. It's the one I saw off the Bight earlier on.'

Belinda squinted at it through her glasses. 'How do you know?'

'I looked at it through the binoculars. Same name. *Van Dijk*.'

As they watched the boat tie up, they saw Paul and Tiffany coming along the street. Tracy was with them. She and Paul were deep in conversation about something.

Tiffany was walking slightly apart from the other two, and looked decidedly miffed. Perhaps that was why she greeted Holly and Belinda more warmly than she had done the day before.

'Did you know there's a funfair at the other end of the town?' she said. 'They've got some fabulous rides . . . Pirate Ship, Moon Ride . . . everything. A sort of mini Disney World without the queues. Everyone says it's fantastic.'

Her brother grinned. 'Everyone. That means the two guys on the boat next to ours. I wouldn't mind going to have a look at it though. How about you three?'

'Great.' Belinda hadn't been to many fairgrounds. They weren't exactly her snobbish mother's favourite places.

'Yeah. It's time we had a break,' Holly said. After all, it was supposed to be a holiday, and things were getting a bit heavy. A day at the fair would do them all good.

While they were having their favourite chocolate nut sundaes, they saw two members of the crew of the foreign yacht come ashore. They were joined at the quayside by another man, slightly older, in a suit rather than the sweater and jeans that the others were wearing.

Holly stared at him, then nudged Tracy. 'Isn't

that the guy that came into the cove with the powerboat?' she said. 'Not Scarface; the other one.'

Tracy looked. 'It's hard to say. They were wearing that mad scientist gear, but I think so.'

Paul's eyes followed their gaze. 'That's the estate agent,' he said. 'The one who warned us about the anthrax.'

The hair on the back of Holly's neck tingled. 'Martyn Hare?'

'Yeah.'

Of course. That's where they'd seen him before. When he had that fearsome row with Carole on their first night. *Was* he the man in the powerboat? Holly tried to imagine what he would look like, dressed in those white overalls and boots.

Paul went back to talking about the funfair. 'You can leave your bikes on our boat,' he suggested. 'It'll be safer than leaving them here.'

They had to pass the foreign yacht to get to the one that Paul and Tiffany were on. '*Van Dijk*,' Holly said. 'I wonder where it comes from.'

'Holland,' Tiffany said.

'How do you know?'

'If you knew anything about sailing, you'd know,' Tiffany said scornfully. 'Look, it says "Amsterdam" under the name. That's its port of registry, and it's flying the Dutch flag.'

Holly felt her anger rise, but said nothing. There was no point in starting a row.

'You don't have to be like that,' Belinda said mildly. 'The paint is flaking badly. I can hardly read it. I didn't recognise the Dutch flag either. We're not all brilliant like you.'

Tiffany went red. 'Sorry,' she muttered.

They could hear the music a mile away . . . a wheezy mixture of oompah bands, pop songs, and carousels strung together with shouts from fairground barkers.

Holly felt a shiver of excitement. 'It's ages since I've been to a fairground,' she said.

They went on the Pirate Ship, and the Water Chute and had a go at the rifle range and the Hoopla stall. But though Holly was thoroughly enjoying herself, a part of her mind was trying to piece together the puzzle that was becoming more and more complicated. There were so many loose ends; she couldn't make out whether they belonged in the picture or not. Was it coincidence that the yacht that was now moored in Framley Harbour was the same one that had been anchored near the island this morning? And where did Martyn Hare fit into all this?

After about an hour, the group broke up and Holly and Belinda had left the others and were now on their own, watching a music video in one of the arcades.

'Let's go,' Belinda said. 'There's no air in here.'

'In a minute,' Holly said. 'I really like this song.'

Belinda shook her head. 'I want to go now.'

Holly was puzzled. It wasn't like Belinda to be so awkward. Perhaps she wasn't feeling well. She did look slightly pale. 'OK.'

They struggled through the crowd and came out. It was cooler here, and they wandered along towards the Hall of Mirrors. Then suddenly, as they passed a café, Belinda practically dragged her inside.

'I'm starving. Let's have an ice cream.'

Holly wrinkled her nose. 'Another one? Already?'

'I'll treat you,' Belinda insisted.

Reluctantly, Holly let herself be persuaded. Belinda was behaving most oddly, she thought.

When they got back out again she found out why. 'Come on, Belinda,' Holly said. 'Why do you keep lagging behind?'

'I think someone's watching us. The man in the navy sweater.'

Holly glanced over her shoulder. There were so many people. 'I can't see anyone in a navy sweater.'

Belinda swung round. 'He's gone again.'

'What do you mean?'

'He was in the tent where Paul and Tracy were. Then I thought we'd dodged him, but I saw him again when we got to the café. That's why I dragged you inside. And I've seen him since. It's the man from the fish market.'

'The Spaniard?'

'I'm not sure. He's keeping well behind. But he's always there.'

Holly thought for a minute. 'Quick. We'll go in the Hall of Mirrors. You watch for him while I get the tickets.'

The two girls ran up the steps, and Belinda scanned the crowd whilst Holly bought two tickets. Then they raced inside.

Panting with fear, they stood with their backs against the inner wall. After a few minutes, Holly breathed a sigh of relief. 'Looks like we gave him the slip. Let's see if we can get out another way.'

It was on their way out that they saw Tiffany. She was looking into a mirror and laughing and giggling like crazy with the two sailors from the Dutch yacht.

'What are you doing here?' she demanded.

'Same as you. Having fun,' Holly said.

'You are a friend of Tiffany?' The taller of the two men stared boldly at Holly. He spoke good English, though with an American accent. Holly guessed he was in his early twenties, with fair hair and a tanned complexion. He wasn't bad looking, yet there was something about him that set her teeth on edge.

She didn't answer.

He took a long drag on the cigarette he was smoking. It was a funny shape – as if he had rolled it himself. It had a strange smell, too. An alarm bell rang in Holly's head.

'We're going to look for Paul and Tracy,' she said, looking at Tiffany. 'Coming?'

Tiffany hesitated, then turned to the two sailors. 'I have to go. Will you be here tomorrow?'

'We leave for Holland tonight,' the other one said. He winked. 'Much money. Back in two days.'

The taller man gave him a warning glance, and muttered something in Dutch.

By the time they found Paul and Tracy, Tiffany had regained her good mood. They all walked back to the harbour, laughing and joking about the good time they'd had.

'See you tomorrow,' the girls called, and set off to Aunt Carole's.

When they got home, Holly got out the Mystery Club notebook. 'Those guys said the ship was sailing tonight, didn't they?'

'That's right,' Belinda said. 'Why?'

'If that was cannabis those guys were smoking, then maybe they brought a load of it in this morning, and now they're going back to Holland for some more.'

Belinda's eyes widened. 'Maybe that's what the

85

shorter one meant when he said "much money".
You could see the other guy was trying to shut
him up.'

'You've got it.' Holly was writing as fast as she
could. 'They wouldn't bring the drugs into the
harbour in case they were searched by Customs.
But if they dropped them off on the island, then
they could be brought over to the cove when it
got dark.'

'Do you mean tonight?' Belinda asked. 'They're
going to collect them tonight?'

Holly nodded. 'I think so.'

Tracy's eyes shone with excitement. 'Wow! Let's
go for it.'

'Oh, no,' Belinda said with a sigh. 'Not another
night without sleep!'

7   Caught!

Holly helped Carole get dinner ready while Belinda
was reading in the other room, and Tracy was
practising the violin upstairs. The TV set was
on in the kitchen and the main story on the
news was about a drugs seizure at a house in
Sheffield. Customs and police officers had been
given a tip-off, and a large amount of cannabis had
been found, with a street value of half a million
pounds. 'Police believe that the drugs are coming
into this country from Holland,' the reporter said.
'Ports and airports along the northeast coast of
Britain are under surveillance.'

That settled it in Holly's mind. Framley was on
the northeast coast. It must be drugs. It all added
up. She decided to tell Carole what the Mystery
Club had found out so far. 'We saw a Dutch
boat in the harbour this morning,' she said. 'It
was anchored off Anthrax Island earlier on.'

'I wish you wouldn't call it that,' Carole said.
'That was during wartime, more than fifty years
ago.'

'Yes, and it's safe now. Decontaminated.'

Carole smiled sadly. 'We don't know that for sure. Anthrax spores can lie dormant for a very long time.'

'But we do know,' Holly said. 'I went to see the coastguards and they told me the island was declared safe more than a month ago.'

'I think you must have misunderstood,' said Carole. 'If anything like that had happened the whole town would be buzzing. It would have been in the newspapers.'

They were getting off the point. 'There's going to be a public announcement at the end of the month,' Holly said impatiently. 'Anyway, it's definitely safe now.'

'What does this have to do with the Dutch boat?' Carole asked.

'I'm trying to tell you. I think it's bringing canna-bis in from Holland and landing it on the island.'

A smile lifted the corner of her aunt's mouth. 'Your father warned me about your vivid imagin-ation, Holly. Just because the news mentions drugs coming in from Holland it doesn't mean that every Dutch person you see is a smuggler.'

Holly felt her cheeks go red. If Carole didn't take her seriously, what chance would they have of convincing the police? They'd have to get more evidence.

High tide was at nine o'clock. Holly had checked

in the local paper. It would be getting dark by then. If she was right about the Dutchmen smuggling drugs to the island this morning, then someone would be ferrying them across to the cove tonight.

And this time we're going to be there, she thought.

Carole put a hand on her arm. 'Sorry if I hurt your feelings, Holly. It's just that Framley is far too quiet a place to have smugglers or anything like that. I don't think people would recognise cannabis if it was waved under their noses. Not here.'

But that's exactly the sort of place for smugglers to choose, Holly thought. *A place where no one would suspect*.

After the evening meal, the three girls sat in the upstairs sitting-room, drinking cocoa and working out their plan.

'It's no good waiting till we see the lights,' Tracy said. 'Even with the bikes we wouldn't get to the Bight in time. And we might run straight into them.'

'Carole will never let us stay out all night,' Belinda said.

Tracy and Holly stared at her. 'We're not going to tell her, silly,' said Tracy.

'Besides, it won't be all night,' Holly said. 'An hour should do it. If we haven't seen the lights by the time the tide starts going back we might as well come home.'

Holly took their mugs downstairs. Her aunt was watching television, the door to the hallway wide open. She'd have to find an excuse to close it. 'Is it good?' she asked, on her way back from the kitchen.

Carole nodded, her eyes still on the screen. 'A murder mystery. It's only just started. You lot coming down to watch?'

Holly hesitated. 'No, thanks. Not tonight.'

Her aunt turned round in surprise. 'Why not? I thought you three were mystery-mad.'

'We are. It's just . . .' Just what? What excuse could she give? She hated to lie, and anyway her mind was a blank.

'We're exhausted,' she stammered finally. 'It's all that excitement at the funfair.' Even to herself it sounded pretty weak.

Carole shook her head in disbelief. 'What's wrong? Is it what I said to you earlier?'

'No. Honestly. It's nothing to do with that.' Her heart was pounding. If she didn't come up with a more convincing reason, Carole would be bound to guess they were up to something.

'There's only a few more days of the holiday left.' That was true anyhow. 'We're planning what we're going to do.' That was true too.

Carole shrugged. She didn't look convinced but it would have to do.

Holly closed the living-room door, collected their

90

anoraks from the cupboard and went upstairs. It was nearly a quarter to nine. They'd better hurry.

'Seen anything yet?' she asked Tracy, who was sitting by the window.

'Nope. But I've got my stopwatch ready. Maybe if we time the whole thing exactly we might be able to crack the code.'

'Good thinking. Is everyone ready?'

Belinda and Tracy nodded silently, clearly nervous.

They tiptoed downstairs, hearts thudding. The back door squeaked as they opened it, and they froze. But Carole didn't seem to hear.

Squeezing themselves flat against the wall, they edged round to the garage. This was going to be the tricky bit.

'Lift the door up off the floor as you open it,' Tracy whispered. 'Don't let it scrape on the gravel. I'll get your bike.'

Slowly and carefully Holly opened the battered wooden door, then closed it after them as they took out the bikes. They carried the bikes over the lawn instead of using the path, so Carole wouldn't hear them.

'Whew!' Belinda said, as they reached the road. 'Any second I was expecting to hear her yell at us. How are we going to get back? What if she locks us out?'

The three friends looked at one another, horrified. 'I never thought of that,' Holly admitted. 'Oh, well . . . it's too late now. We'll worry about that when we get back.'

They left the bikes at the Bight, where the road petered out into dunes and marram grass. They tucked them between a couple of gorse bushes. It was dusk, and there was no one about. The gate to the Grange was firmly padlocked, and there was no sign of life at Wetherby's Farm. There weren't even any lights.

'I expect she's in bed,' Holly said. 'People go to bed early in the country. She probably has to be up at dawn to milk the cows.'

'Pity we didn't think to bring a hot drink,' Belinda said as they plodded up the cliff towards the spot where they had seen the cove. 'It may be a long wait.'

Before anyone could reply, there was a flicker of light from the island.

With a sense of excitement bubbling up inside, Holly grabbed the binoculars. 'Quick. Someone make a note of this. Belinda?'

'I'm ready.'

'Tracy?'

'Got it.' Tracy set her stopwatch.

Methodically, they watched and timed the signal. After the flicker there was a pause, then a white flash, followed by a green one, and another white flash followed by a red.

The answering signal came from almost beneath their feet. One . . . two . . . three green, and a longer flash of white.

'Wow,' Tracy breathed. 'They're right here. In the cove.'

'What do we do now?' Belinda whispered.

Holly put her fingers to her lips. 'Shh . . .'

She motioned to them to move into the cover of the bracken. It was stiff and spiky and the green fronds tickled their noses, making them want to sneeze. Holly scanned the island.

Perhaps if it hadn't been twilight, she might have been able to see more clearly. But even as she watched, she saw that a boat was already making its way across the mile-long stretch of water between the island and the mainland. Belinda was right, she thought. It *did* seem to appear out of nowhere. It was as if the cliffs had opened up and spat it out.

They stared at the tiny shape in the deepening grey between sky and sea. It hardly seemed real – just a pale swirl in their line of vision. Holly blinked, straining to follow its path as the light faded. Soon it would be here. And they would at last see what kind of cargo it held.

The three friends held their breath. All their

concentration, all their thoughts were focused on one little boat.

Suddenly, out of the silence came a deep-throated growl that stopped the breath in their throats. There was a flurry of movement in the bracken, and a man's voice shouted a command.

'Prince! Stay.'

The dog stood guard a few feet away from them, the fur on the back of his neck standing up like a ruff. He looked enormous, and dangerous. The girls didn't dare move.

A man moved out of the shadows. 'I might have guessed it was you.' Thomas Clough's eyes were dark with anger. 'You're lucky you didn't get shot.'

Defiantly, Holly looked him straight in the eyes. 'We're not on your property, Mr Clough. We have every right to be here, without expecting to get shot.'

He glared at her for a moment. Then, unexpectedly, the beginnings of a smile curved the corners of his mouth. 'That aunt of yours isn't the only tough lady in the family. Does she know you're out on the Bight at this time of night?'

Holly hesitated.

'I see.' The smile became broader. 'She doesn't know.'

'Not exactly.'

'Come on. I'm taking you home.'

94

Home? Whose home? Holly's mind grasshoppered from imprisonment at the Grange to a confrontation with Carole. One would be almost as bad as the other. 'We've got our bikes, thank you,' she snapped.

'You can put them in the van. We're getting this sorted out once and for all. Come on.'

The journey back was silent. He stood by, watching as they walked their bikes to the Grange, followed closely by the Alsatian. Then he bundled them – bikes and all – into the van. 'You sit in the front with me,' he commanded, looking at Holly.

Prince went to jump into the van too, but Thomas Clough ordered him to stay. Reluctantly the dog stood back and watched the van move away.

When they pulled into the driveway at Tumble Avenue, Carole came out on to the front porch, looking anxious.

Thomas Clough got out of the van and walked towards her while the girls lifted the bikes out of the back. 'I've rescued your niece and her friends for the second time, Miss Earnshaw,' he said. 'Can't you keep these girls under control?'

Carole bristled. Drawing herself up to her full height she asked, 'If I remember correctly, Mr Clough, you merely allowed them to telephone me and remain under your roof until I picked them up. Kind of you, but hardly a rescue.' Her voice was icy. 'What did you rescue them from this time?'

His attitude softened slightly. 'They were up on the cliffs above the Bight. Not only is it very isolated up there, but there have been some strange characters hanging around lately. Highly unwise for three kids to be on their own in the dark.'

'We're not kids,' Holly interrupted. She turned to her aunt. 'He had a gun. He said we could have been shot.'

'They could indeed,' Thomas Clough said. 'My dog and I were out hunting foxes.'

It sounded reasonable. Holly took a good look at him – not that you could tell a criminal by his looks. But Thomas looked honest enough, and he'd been pretty fair with them too. Not like his brother, Ian. Could he live at Framley Grange and not know about the lights? Could his brother be acting on his own in all this?

Thoughtfully, Holly said, 'Did you know that the island is no longer Ministry of Defence property, Mr Clough?'

'Sure I did. So what?' He looked bewildered at the change of subject.

'Did you know that there are warning notices along the cliff and around your land telling people to keep out because it is Ministry of Defence property?'

A wave of colour flooded up his neck. 'The cliffs are dangerous. There are often rock-falls. If anyone were to be killed or injured . . .' He shrugged.

'We're not insured for that. Ian said they would take more notice if they thought it was connected with the island. Anthrax, you know.' His voice trailed away.

Carole had been silent. 'You deliberately put up notices that you knew were not true?' she asked now.

'The notices were up already. Ian just added a few words. It's not doing any harm,' he pleaded.

'If those notices are not down within forty-eight hours, I'm going to the police. Is that clear?'

'Perfectly.' He got in the van, slammed it into gear and drove off.

Holly turned to her aunt. 'You were terrific. Thanks for standing by us.'

Carole's face was suddenly stony. 'Put your bikes in the garage. Then come into the sitting-room. I want to talk to you. Oh, and I see you have my binoculars. I want to know why you thought you could borrow them without my permission.'

The next half-hour was both painful and embarrassing. Holly didn't try to excuse herself over the binoculars. 'You weren't around when we needed them that first day,' she said, 'and after that we forgot. I'm sorry.'

Carole was upset. She said that she had treated them as responsible adults and they had let her down. Holly had to admit she had a point there.

'But we *had* to go down to the Bight,' she said.

'I needed to find out whether my theory about the Dutch ship was right.'

'Why didn't you explain?'

Holly shook her head stubbornly. 'I tried to tell you. You said I was too suspicious. If I had asked, would you have let us go?'

Reluctantly her aunt had to admit that she wouldn't.

'I told you about the island being decontaminated, and I was going to tell you about the fake notices – but you wouldn't have believed me.'

'You're right. I have always prided myself on being intelligent – quick to catch on to any situation – but this time I couldn't see the very thing that was right under my nose. I'm sorry.

'Oh, by the way,' Carole continued, walking over to the side table and picking up a couple of envelopes, 'these two letters were delivered while you were out. One for you, Tracy, and one for Holly.'

Holly turned over the cheap white envelope. Her name was written in capital letters. HOLLY. Nothing else. Not even a stamp.

Who could be writing to her? And why?

8   Vengeance is mine

Holly slit open the envelope with her thumb. She didn't need to take the whole sheet of paper out. She knew by the first few lines. They were words from a newspaper, roughly cut out and stuck on: YOU DO NOT LISTEN TO MY WARNING . . .

She thrust it back in the envelope and pushed it into her pocket. She'd have to wait until later to tell the others. 'Did you see who delivered them?' she asked casually.

'No. Don't you know who they're from?'

'I do,' Tracy said sadly. 'Paul and Tiffany. They're going home. Their father suddenly got called back for business.'

Luckily, Carole assumed that both letters were from Paul and Tiffany. She looked sympathetically at Belinda. 'Never mind. I'm sure they meant to include you in their goodbyes.'

'It doesn't bother me,' Belinda insisted. 'I didn't like Tiffany a whole lot anyway.'

They curled up in the deep leather armchairs and told Carole what they suspected.

'You seem to have sussed it out pretty well,' Carole said when they had finished. 'What about the lights?'

Belinda put the Mystery Club notebook on the table. 'The first signal was from the island.'

'Flashes of two seconds' duration each,' Tracy said. 'I timed them.'

'As I was saying, one white flash, then a green –'

'Followed by a five second pause,' Tracy interrupted.

'Then a white, then a red.'

Holly took up the story. 'The reply came from the cove right under where we were sitting.' She had been going to tell Carole about the blocked off side alley in the tunnel, but stopped herself just in time.

'There were three green flashes and then a white one,' she said. 'And I think I know what it means.'

Three pairs of eyes looked at her expectantly. 'When you are driving, what does green stand for?' Holly asked.

'Go.'

'And red?'

'Stop.'

'I think the first signal – from the island – is a question meaning "Is it OK to go ahead?" And the answer from the mainland is either, "Go, go, go." Or "No, no, no."'

The others looked at her admiringly. 'Brilliant!' Tracy exclaimed.

'Simple, yet effective,' Carole said. 'Well done, Holly. I'll ring the police.'

'Not yet, please. Let's wait and see whether the Cloughs take down those notices. You said you'd give them forty-eight hours. Then would be a good chance to go to the police and tell them about the lights at the same time.'

Carole looked worried. 'Are you sure you know what you're doing? You promised your father that you'd keep out of trouble, remember?'

'And I will. We all will. We just need that extra bit of time.'

Carole sighed, biting her lip. 'Not a minute longer, then.'

'Thanks.'

Carole yawned, then apologised. 'I'm absolutely shattered. I must go to bed. Goodnight, girls.'

When she had gone, Holly pulled the note from her pocket. Together the three friends looked at the crudely assembled message.

YOU DO NOT LISTEN TO MY WARNING. DO NOT EXPECT MERCY. VENGEANCE IS MINE.

The three girls sat in silence, their throats dry with fear.

Belinda was the first to break the silence. 'That

last bit's from the Bible. I know I've seen it some-where in the last few days.'

Holly agreed. She tried to remember where she had seen or heard the phrase recently.

Suddenly, Belinda's eyes glinted behind her spectacles. Her face lit up with a broad grin. 'I remember,' she said. 'It was on the notice-board of that little church by the coastguards' office. I remember looking at it while I was waiting for you.'

'Of course!' Whoever was watching them from the fish market would have seen it, too. The market was right next to the church. And that's how he knew her name, too. She remembered Belinda calling out to her as she went up the steps to the coastguards' office. It all made sense.

But who was the man?

Tracy went for her usual run along the beach the next morning. She came back looking sad. 'Paul and Tiffany's boat is gone,' she said. 'I'll miss them. Paul was great fun.'

To cheer her up they decided to walk into Framley to look at the shops. The weather was calm and still, and there was a real holiday feeling as they strolled along the High Street towards the harbour.

They looked in the window of Bingley and Hare as they passed. Pictures of houses and flats filled the bottom half of the window, but above them was a clear view into the office.

'Look who's talking to Martyn Hare,' Belinda said. 'And they're not exactly the best of friends either.'

Martyn Hare was seated at his desk, his face pale and angry. As they watched, Ian Clough got up from the chair facing him and banged the desk with his fist. Then he strode out of the office, slamming the door after him.

Keeping their heads down, the girls stared at the window as he strode past them and they heard a vehicle thrust into gear and roar away. The girls dared to take a quick look.

A white Land Rover! Was it the one that had forced them off the road?

'Did you see whether the front was damaged?' Holly asked Tracy.

'No, but I got the number.'

Holly frowned. 'Why didn't I notice it when we passed? I wish I'd seen it.'

'It wouldn't have made much difference,' Belinda insisted. 'He probably wouldn't chance driving round for days with a damaged wing. If Carole had seen it and gone to the police they'd have picked him right up. They could have matched the paintwork on Carole's car to the scratches on his bumper. No, I bet he went to a garage and got it fixed the next day.'

'Good thinking,' Holly said. 'Come on, we've got things to do.'

They continued down the road towards the harbour. The crowds were thicker here. As they passed the Green Dragon pub, a gang of about six youths came stumbling out. The girls dodged to one side and the gang careered across the pavement and crashed against a telephone kiosk.

There was a volley of swear words, and an angry face glared out at them – the phone still in his hand.

'Scarface!' Tracy gasped. 'It's Scarface.'

Quickly, Holly pulled them into a shop doorway. 'You watch him, Belinda. He hasn't seen you before. When he moves, you follow him while Tracy and I go on ahead on the other side of the road. That way he may not notice us.'

At that moment there was a squeal from Belinda. 'He's going. Quick.'

But he wasn't going far. He crossed the road and, after glancing right and left, slipped into the amusement arcade opposite.

'Let's split up,' Holly said. 'Try to keep near him without being seen. We don't know one another. Right? We'll meet back at the café afterwards.'

The three girls sauntered across to the amusement arcade, each one going to a different machine. The place was busy, with so many people round the various machines that the girls found it quite easy to blend into the background.

Scarface was standing near the back of the arcade, leaning against a pillar. His eyes never left the entrance. Holly wondered how she could get nearer to him without being seen. But while she was still working out a plan she saw Martyn Hare stride in through the door. Hastily she joined a group of teenagers at a pinball machine.

Out of the corner of her eye she saw Scarface and Martyn move over to the fruit machines and begin talking, with their backs to the main part of the arcade. Silently, she moved to a video game almost behind them, where a ginger-headed boy of about ten was playing with the utmost concentration.

'You'll have to move it out of there,' Martyn was saying. 'Clough says his brother's getting suspicious.'

Clough! But which one? Holly wondered.

Scarface's reply was just a mumble, but Martyn's angry retort was as clear as day. 'I don't care how you do it. Just do it. Tonight if possible. Use the Spaniard. He's got contacts.'

The Spaniard? So there was a connection. Was he the driver of the crane? she thought. The one in the fish market? At the fairground?

Martyn Hare marched out of the arcade, and to her relief Holly saw Tracy slip out after him. Turning to look for Scarface, she was just in time to see him go through a door at the back of the arcade. Holly hurried after him, and as she turned the handle of the door she heard an angry voice. 'And where do you think you're going?'

Without waiting to answer the question, she slipped through the door and closed it behind her.

The surface of the lane was bumpy and pitted with the tracks of a heavy vehicle. It looked vaguely familiar, but Holly was concentrating on keeping Scarface in view without him seeing her.

I'll worry about where I am later, she thought. Luckily there were plenty of broken-down doors and empty yards along the way, and she sidled from one hiding-place to another without Scarface suspecting that he was being followed.

Suddenly he stopped. Shrinking against the wall, Holly watched as he gave a piercing whistle and stood waiting – looking expectantly at one of the doorways in a high wall on the opposite side of the lane.

For a long time nothing happened. He gave another shrill whistle, and in the still air Holly heard sounds of a bolt being drawn back. Then the door opened.

'About time,' Scarface snarled, and disappeared.

With thudding heart, Holly tiptoed up and put her ear to the door. Not a sound. She tried the handle and felt it give. Inch by inch she opened the door, afraid that at any moment it would be yanked from her grasp and she would be faced by . . . whom?

But all was silent. All she could see as she peered inside were two big packing cases with a familiar logo. Of course. The scrapyard! She should have guessed. But where was Scarface now? She peeped round the side of the cases and looked up at the window of the Portakabin.

Scarface and Ian Clough were talking. Arguing, it looked like – but Holly was too far away to hear what was being said. There was nothing more she could do here. Not on her own anyway. Holly crept back to the door, closed it carefully behind her and made her escape.

As she walked towards the meeting place they had arranged, she tried to work out what it all meant. If Ian was talking to Scarface, that seemed to let Thomas out in the clear.

But Thomas was getting suspicious, they had said. Of what? Something that was going to have to be moved. And the Spaniard was going to help move it. What could it be? And even more important – where was it now?

When Holly got back to the café, Tracy and Belinda were already there. She got herself a cup of tea and joined them at the table. 'Where did he go?' she asked. 'Did you manage to keep up with him?'

Tracy nodded. 'It was easy as pie. He only went back to his office. What about you?'

Holly told them about the lane, and her discovery that the back entrance to the scrapyard was almost opposite the back entrance of the amusement arcade. 'They're going to be moving something. Tonight, if possible. We've got to find out what it is.'

'How?' said Tracy.

'Anyone know how to handle a boat?' asked Holly.

'What kind of boat?' Tracy looked puzzled.

'I don't know. The sort of boat we might to able to hire.'

'We used to have a yacht,' Belinda said. 'The outfit had a tender and I often used that.'

'A tender? You mean a boat of some kind?'

'Yes. Ours was a little rubber dinghy, with an outboard motor. Do you mean something like that?'

'That'll do nicely.' Holly grinned. 'Are you sure you could manage one?'

Belinda nodded. 'Sure, no problem. But where are we going?'

'It's like this,' Holly went on. 'Martyn Hare is busy in his office. So he's safely occupied. Ian Clough is in the scrapyard with Scarface. There's only the Spaniard and Thomas to worry about.' Holly's eyes sparkled with mischief. 'This might be an ideal time to pay a visit to Anthrax Island.'

9   An exciting discovery

There were plenty of notices around the harbour, with seamen only too pleased to persuade people to sail around the bay. But no one wanted to hire out a boat to three teenagers – and girls at that.

'It's positively sexist,' Tracy exploded, after the third one they approached said it would be different if they had a boy with them. 'It's not our age, it's because we're *girls*.'

There was only one more place to try. A notice in big red letters said BOATS FOR HIRE. The owner sat on a pile of fishing nets, watching their efforts with considerable amusement.

'Having a bit of trouble?' he said as they walked towards him.

This time it was Belinda who took over. 'We want to hire a dinghy. For two hours, please. Not the small ones. I want the twelve footer – the one with the Suzuki outboard engine.'

He looked at her with heightened interest. 'You certainly know what you want, girl. And what size of engine would you be looking for?' he asked slyly.

'It's a five horsepower, isn't it?'

'An' it's right you are now.' The man gave her a hint of a smile. 'I suppose you'd know how to start it all right?'

Belinda snorted. 'Simple. Turn on the fuel and pull-start. Now, can we have it?'

His eyes narrowed. 'Don't be in too much of a hurry. If you were sailing into shallow water what would you do?'

'Tilt it up before we got there.'

'Right y'are then. You've passed the test, girl. Got your own boat, have you?'

Belinda shook her head. 'Not now. We used to. And I've got a few questions I want to ask you before we take it out.'

'Have you indeed?' The man grinned at her, clearly amused by her confidence.

'Where are the life-jackets? We'll want oars, too. I take it there's plenty of fuel? And a spare can?'

'All present and correct. Peter O'Keefe never hires his boats out without the necessary gear. But you're right to ask. So, if you've got the money you can have my boat with pleasure.'

The girls paid him, put on the life-jackets and settled themselves in the boat. With casual skill, Belinda switched on the petrol, gave her some choke, and with a sharp pull on the cord they were off.

As they eased out of the harbour and into the bay, the wind lifted their hair, blowing strands across their faces and stinging their breath with a mixture of salty spray and petrol fumes. The sea, though calm as oil inside the sea wall, now slapped against the boat with noisy hands.

Tracy took a deep breath. 'This is brilliant. Why didn't we do this before? Everything looks so different from here.'

Holly raised her voice over the noise of the engine. 'I didn't know you could handle a boat like this, Belinda. Why didn't you say?'

Belinda shrugged, keeping her eyes straight ahead. 'I didn't know it was anything special.'

Holly laughed. 'You always say it's nothing special. Don't you *ever* blow your own trumpet?'

Belinda grinned happily. 'Only about horses.'

It wasn't long before they were near enough to the island to need to look for a place to land. The side facing Fram Bight was impossible. Tall cliffs full of nesting sea birds rose sheer from a sea awash with white foam.

In spite of being certain that it was now safe, Holly's heart beat faster when she saw that the wartime notices still ringed the island.

THIS ISLAND IS GOVERNMENT PROPERTY
UNDER EXPERIMENT.
THE GROUND IS CONTAMINATED WITH
ANTHRAX AND IS DANGEROUS.
LANDING IS PROHIBITED
BY ORDER.

111

Tracy shuddered. 'I'm not surprised that nobody wants to come here.'

The wind seemed suddenly colder than it had been, the sky less blue. 'I daren't move in any closer,' Belinda said. 'What now, Holly?'

'There's bound to be somewhere to land. Let's keep going – even if we have to go right round it.'

Suddenly Holly gave a sharp gasp. 'No wonder you said that the powerboat appeared like magic when we were in the cove. Look!'

It was as if a giant had taken a bite out of the cliffs, leaving two knife edges of rock jutting out at either side. The space between them was wide enough to take a boat comfortably. Stretched across the opening from cliff top to just above sea level was a huge camouflage net.

The girls stared up at it in stunned silence. At last, Tracy spoke. 'Wow! You'd never see that unless you were looking for it.'

'Or in too close for comfort,' Belinda said dryly. 'This is dangerous. If I get caught in the swell we'll be on those rocks and well and truly in trouble. I'm going to have to move away a bit.'

Gradually, the island tapered down to sea level and they saw a small sheltered bay, with a sandy beach and an old wooden jetty that looked as if it had been recently repaired and renewed.

'This will do,' said Holly. 'Can you take her in here?'

They landed as close to the beach as they could, tied up to the jetty, and scrambled out.

There was something eerie about the island. A silence. A sense of terrible sadness.

The girls walked up the beach, past the sand and the pebbles and up the pathway to where the grass began. No one spoke. Their throats were tight, their muscles taut.

A road of sorts led inland. Heather fringed the edges, stretching away up the slope and into the distance. It should have been pretty, but somehow it wasn't. There wasn't a trace of a bird or an animal to be seen. Even the sea birds they had seen on the cliffs did not venture this far.

Tracy gave a shuddering sigh. 'I don't like it.'

'Neither do I,' Holly said quietly. 'If you two want to wait for me in the boat, I'll be as quick as I can.'

Belinda shook her head stubbornly. 'I'm going with you.'

'Tracy?'

'OK. Count me in.'

Above the beach were a couple of fishermen's cottages, roofless now – their rafters blackened by fire, the windows blank and open to sea and sky. Inside, grass was growing through the paved floors but that too was distorted – stunted by lack of light and clean air.

Subdued, the Mystery Club followed the road up the hill. When they got to the top they found themselves looking down into a shallow valley ringed with hills. This looked a little more normal – though it too must have been abandoned more than fifty years ago. There were more houses here, perhaps eleven or twelve; it was difficult to tell. Some were little more than a ruined pattern of stone walls. Others had survived better.

There were three at the crossroads of what must have been the centre of the village, opposite the ruins of a tiny church. These cottages looked in a much better state. The girls walked down the hill towards them.

Tracy shook her head. 'Eleven families used to live here. Thirty people at least. I wonder what happened to them?'

Holly sighed. 'They must have hated leaving their homes. I bet some of them were born here.' *Did they know what the place was going to be used for?* she wondered. It was a horrible thought. 'What'll we do?' she asked. 'Take one cottage each? Or stick together?'

'Stick together!' The decision was unanimous.

Holly pushed open the door of the nearest cottage. To her surprise it felt warm. Lived in. There were the remains of a fire in the grate. A chair and a table were near the window. A buzz of excitement ran up her spine.

She stood in the doorway. 'Try the next one, Tracy.'

Tracy tried it. The door swung open and she peered inside. Looking across at Holly, she said, 'It's full of stores. All sorts of things. Shall I try the end one?'

Holly nodded.

Her words, when they came, were electrifying. 'There's a portable generator in here. And lights. Powerful ones. With red and green filters. And in the yard there's a pick-up truck. Like there was at the Grange.'

She held her hand up to stop them interrupting. 'There's even a sort of telescope on a tripod.' She turned to Belinda. 'You said you'd seen someone looking at us through a telescope when you were up on the cliffs at the Bight.'

Wow! This made their journey worthwhile. Now they could go to the police. This was what detective work was all about. Holy felt ten feet tall. Beavering away at a problem until you solved it.

Then cold reason set in. They hadn't solved it. Not yet. There was no law against signalling to your friends. OK, maybe the men were trespassing on the island, but that wasn't much of a crime. There must be more to it.

'We'll have to search the cottages,' she said. 'Find

115

out what these guys are carrying . . . when the next load is coming in . . . information about the operation . . . anything. Let's start with the one with the stores.'

Most of the stuff was very ordinary. Sugar, butter, bread, potatoes. And then, tucked away on their own were several packing cases with a logo on them. A curved logo of a red knot on green. The same strange logo they had seen behind the shed at the scrapyard.

Holly stared at them, frowning. They weren't very big. About the size of a bale of hay, that's all. 'If only we knew what was in them.'

'Couldn't we prise them open? There's sure to be a knife or two in the other house,' Belinda said.

Holly shook her head. 'We don't want them to know we're on to them. They might pack up the whole operation. Then we'll have lost them.'

They carried on searching the cottage. But there was nothing else of importance. The bedrooms were dank and unfurnished. No one had lived here recently, that was for sure.

When they came downstairs again Holly tried shaking the cases to see if they rattled, but they felt pretty solid.

Tracy watched her curiously. 'What are you doing?'

'If it was full of guns, they might rattle about. How long do you figure a rifle is?'

Belinda shook her head. 'They'd be packed with straw. They'd never move. It's got to fool the Customs and Excise if they came aboard the ship.'

That was a thought. Somehow the crooks would have to get the cases from one boat to another, and then to the island without arousing suspicion. How? Holly had heard of ships being boarded and inspected by the Customs whilst they were at sea. That meant the smuggled goods must look like a genuine cargo. The more she thought about it, the more certain she was that it was drugs. But how to prove it? That was the difficult part.

As they turned to come out of the cottage another part of the jigsaw slotted into place. On a hook behind the door hung two white overalls, with trousers and hoods to match.

'There are our crazy scientists,' Holly laughed. 'Look, they've even got gas masks, though I doubt if they work. Still, it's a good disguise. One more house to go. Come on.'

Tracy was looking uneasy. 'We've been here too long. Someone is living here. How do we know he won't come back? Down in this hollow we're like easy targets. The first thing we'd see would be old Scarface marching in at the front door. One of us ought to be standing guard.'

She was right. 'Who do you suggest?' Holly asked. 'You?'

'No. You and I can run fast once we get the

message. Belinda isn't as quick. And she's the best one for the boat. How loud can you shout, Belinda?'

'I can do better than that.' Belinda put two fingers in her mouth and blew. An ear-splitting whistle rang through the house.

'That'll do nicely.' Holly grinned. 'Where did you learn to do that?'

Belinda looked pleased with herself. 'Not bad, is it? Meltdown comes galloping up when he hears it, even if he's down in the end paddock. One of the gardeners taught me to do it when I was about ten. Mum was furious.'

Holly laughed. She could just imagine the refined Mrs Hayes' look of disapproval. 'OK,' she said. 'Back to business. Who's got the binoculars?'

The three girls looked at one another. 'Oh, no!' Holly wailed. 'You don't mean nobody thought to bring them?' She waited a few seconds. 'You *do* mean nobody thought of them.' She shrugged philosophically. 'We'll have to manage without.'

'No. Wait a minute.' Tracy dashed into the end cottage, coming back with the telescope on a folded tripod. 'This should be pretty powerful. If he could see us in the cove, you'll be able to see anyone coming over in a boat. Go on, Belinda. Quick!'

Holly gave her some hasty instructions. 'Set it up on top of the hill, where we landed. If you see anyone coming, give us a whistle. Then leg it down

118

to the boat and get ready to shoot off as soon as we arrive. OK?'

Without wasting any more time, Belinda tucked the telescope under her arm and jogged away.

Holly and Tracy began to make a search of the main premises. Behind the door was a map of the island like the one at the scrapyard.

There's something different, Holly thought . . . What was it?

She scrutinised the map again. There was a cross inked in red that she didn't remember seeing before. It was out at sea, perhaps a quarter of a mile beyond the island.

I wonder what that's for? she thought.

Beside the map was the month's tide table. Certain days had the high tide highlighted in yellow, with a question mark beside them. The last one for this month was the day after tomorrow. If this meant what she thought it did, they hadn't much time. They were going back home to Willow Vale at the end of the week. If they hadn't solved the mystery by then, they'd never have another chance.

Tracy was upstairs. 'Hey, come and look at this.'

Holly took the stairs two at a time. The tiny bedroom had a stale, tobacco smell. Her eyes took in the untidy clutter of the room. A camp-bed, with a sleeping-bag on top, an empty packing case with an

119

ashtray, a lighter and a packet of cigarette papers on top. In the corner, a pile of clothes and a backpack. That was all. Except for a partly smoked cigarette in the ashtray that looked as if it had been hastily pinched and put out. Not an ordinary cigarette. It was a joint. A joint of cannabis.

Holly examined the packing case again. It had the same curved logo. Just because the top had obviously been opened and it was being used as a table didn't mean it had to be empty.

With a pounding heart, Holly took the things off the top and put them on the bed, trying to remember their exact arrangement.

She lifted the flap and peered in as a whistle – as shrill as a scream – pierced the still air . . .

10 A close call

There was no time now to worry about how the various things had been set out. Holly closed up the packing case and plonked the ash-tray, lighter and papers on top. Then she and Tracy fled downstairs and out of the door.

They pelted back the way they had come, thankful that they had sent Belinda to stand guard. How much time did they have? Would they make it to the boat before someone arrived?

'When they see the telescope they'll know we've been here,' Tracy panted.

Holly could barely speak. Her lungs felt as if they would burst. Her legs felt heavy, and made of rubber. 'If they don't catch us first,' she managed to gasp.

Belinda was in the dinghy, the engine running. 'Careful how you get in,' she said quickly, 'or you'll tip it.'

Holly had a stitch. The pain doubled her up. She bent over, trying to get her breath back. 'You first,' she told Tracy, clutching her side. Then as her friend sat down, she took a deep breath and stepped into the boat.

The engine suddenly deepened in tone, and with a surge of power they were off. 'I'll go round behind the island,' Belinda said, over the noise of the engine. 'Keep your fingers crossed that they haven't heard or seen us. Their boat is much more powerful than ours. They'd easily catch us.'

The pain was easing now, and Holly looked behind them. The sun was already sliding down towards the horizon, and the sea was silver grey, with a slight mist rising from it. She couldn't see anything, and the motor drowned the noise of anything else.

'Had they already started sailing across when you whistled?' she asked.

'No. I didn't wait for that. I saw the boat come out from the cove and figured they must be coming here, so I whistled and ran down to the beach to get the dinghy ready.'

Holly nodded. 'It was the best thing to do. OK, keep going.'

It was dusk when they got back to the house. Carole was waiting for them. 'I thought we'd eat out tonight, girls. How do you fancy Chinese?'

'Brilliant! My favourite,' Belinda said.

'What *isn't* your favourite?' Tracy teased.

'Come on, then. The restaurant gets awfully crowded later on.'

Holly looked down at her T-shirt and jeans. In their flight from the island she had somehow managed to get oil all down one side. 'I look a mess. Mind if I have a shower and change first? Ten minutes – that's all I need.'

'And me,' Tracy and Belinda chorused.

Together they raced upstairs. It was a mad dash, with the three girls joking and giggling as they hurried to get ready.

While she was brushing her hair into some sort of order, Holly glanced out of the window. A dark blue car on the opposite side of the road caught her attention. Its windows were heavily tinted, and she couldn't see anyone inside. But as she looked, the driver's window was wound down and a braceleted hand tossed out a cigarette end.

For a moment she felt uneasy. That was a man's hand, and she'd seen someone wearing a gold bracelet like that somewhere before. But where?

Ten minutes later, the girls piled into Carole's car. Holly was now wearing a crisp pair of chinos and a flame-coloured sports shirt. Tracy's white tailored shorts showed off her tanned legs, and the navy and white striped top emphasised the gold of her hair. Even Belinda had changed out of her old green sweatshirt and jeans and was wearing a new blue tracksuit.

As they pulled out of the driveway, Holly saw the car with the tinted windows move smoothly away from the pavement. All the way to Framley, Holly kept glancing behind. The other car was always there – often two or three cars behind them, but never completely out of sight.

'Is something wrong?' Carole asked as they pulled into the car park outside the restaurant. 'You're very edgy.'

'There's a car following us,' Holly said. 'It was waiting in Tumble Avenue, and it's followed us all the way.'

Carole laughed as she got out of the car. 'Why should anybody follow us, Holly? This isn't Miami. This is sleepy old Framley.'

Holly flushed. 'But I saw it.'

'OK. Where is it now?' Carole asked, looking around.

Holly turned her head from one side to the other. The car park was still as a painted picture – each car silent and empty. She bit her lip. 'It was, really.'

Her aunt patted her on the shoulder. 'Well, we got here safely, anyway.'

The restaurant was furnished in burgundy and gold, with beaded curtains to shield the side booths from prying eyes. Tall vases beside each pillar held exotic plants and spidery bamboo, and the smell of oriental spices hung in the air.

The waiter came up to them. 'Miss Earnshaw?' he asked. 'Your table is waiting. This way.' He led them to a table beside an archway, then handed them a menu each.

As Holly studied it she suddenly realised how hungry she was. They'd skipped lunch, and now it was almost eight o'clock. She didn't see the two men approaching their table.

'Good evening, Miss Earnshaw.'

They all looked up. It was Thomas Clough who had spoken, but the one that Holly was looking at was his brother. He was wearing a lightweight suit, and below the cuff on his right wrist hung a heavy gold bracelet, exactly like the one she had seen on the driver discarding his cigarette.

Why were they there? Holly remembered the conversation she had overheard in the amusement arcade. Was it an alibi while they moved the drugs to a different location? And if Ian Clough was the driver of the car, whose side was Thomas on? She couldn't make Thomas out at all.

While Carole and Thomas were talking, Ian and the three girls looked at one another. The silence was as menacing as anything he could have said. His mouth was a thin line and his eyes were cold.

The waiter came to take their order. Thomas

excused himself as the two brothers were shown to a booth behind a concealing bead curtain.

'He seems quite pleasant,' Carole said. 'A bit rough, but honest, I should say. I can hardly believe all that Mrs Wetherby has to say about them.'

Holly felt confused. When she had first heard about Mrs Wetherby it sounded as if she were a helpless old lady caught up in something she couldn't handle. Yet the glimpse they'd had of her driving a herd of cows had given the impression of her being thoroughly able to look after herself, no matter what.

Maybe it's time to visit Mrs Wetherby, Holly said to herself. They had better do it soon. If that notice in the cottage on the island were to be believed, tomorrow would be their last chance.

As they were finishing their meal, Holly saw the Spaniard come in. Ducking her head so he wouldn't see her, she saw the waiter point towards the booth where Ian and Thomas were seated. The Spaniard hurried over and slipped behind the beaded curtain.

What's he doing here? Holly thought as she finished her dessert.

'That feels better,' Carole said, leaning back. 'I was certainly ready for dinner. How about you girls? Had enough?'

'Yes, thanks. That was fabulous,' Belinda said.

126

Tracy sighed with satisfaction and pushed her chair back. 'I couldn't eat another thing.'

The three men were still inside the booth when Carole paid the bill and the girls followed her outside. Darkness had fallen, but the air was still warm. Though there was no moon, the lights from the harbour twinkled on the water, adding an air of mysterious pleasure to the scene.

They stood at the entrance to the car park. 'What would you like to do now, girls?' Carole asked. 'Go for a walk? See a film? Visit the funfair?'

'We've already been,' Belinda said, 'but it wasn't much fun. Tiffany was with us, and she was a bit of a drag. I didn't like her at all.'

'So you've said.' Carole grinned. 'So I gather you'd like to have another go at the fairground? In that case, we'll get the car. It'll save walking back later. You can get some funny types around that sort of place.'

Earlier on, when they had arrived at the car park, the floodlight had been on although it was still daylight. Now it was off, the glass smashed.

'Typical,' Carole snorted. 'Things are never there when you need them.'

Lights from the road and the restaurant illuminated the first few cars, but beyond that it was dark. In spite of the carefree atmosphere of the evening, Holly felt on edge. A shiver raised the hair on the back of her neck. The others were still laughing and talking, but she couldn't help feeling uneasy.

The purring of an engine was her first warning. It came from the seaward end of the car park, and Holly sensed rather than saw a dark shape in the blackness moving along the line of cars. The engine was as quiet as a tiger stalking a deer, and before she had time to react, a blaze of lights blinded them. With a surge of power the car came roaring towards them.

Holly screamed. She grabbed Belinda's hand and dragged them both into the narrow space between two vehicles. They crouched there – hearts pounding, legs shaking – as the car raced out of the car park, turned the next corner and was gone.

There was a moment's silence, then the three girls picked themselves up. 'Everyone all right?' Holly asked, her voice trembling.

There was a groan, then Carole's voice said, 'Would one of you give me a hand?'

Tracy was there first, but Carole had already scrambled to her feet. 'I've lost a shoe,' she said. 'And my handbag. But at least I'm in one piece.'

'Are you sure you're OK?' Tracy asked anxiously. 'Shall I go over to the restaurant and ask them to call an ambulance?'

Carole shook her head. 'It just caught my elbow, and spun me into one of the parked cars. Good job

128

I was wearing a leather jacket.' She examined the torn sleeve. 'Can someone look for my handbag?'

Tracy tried to persuade her to go back to the restaurant, but Carole shook her head. 'First, I'm going to get you three home,' she said, her voice trembling. 'Then I'm going to phone the police.' She turned to Belinda. 'Sorry about the funfair. Perhaps another night.'

While the other three headed for the car, Holly bent to look for Carole's handbag and shoe. It didn't take long. There in the middle of the track was a shoe, flattened beyond recognition. A few yards further on was a black leather handbag with the imprint of a muddy tyre right across it.

'Someone put the kettle on while I telephone the police,' Carole said when they got home. 'I need a pot of good strong tea.'

She left the handbag and the broken shoe on the hall table, and looked down at her laddered tights. 'I'll go and change,' she said.

By the time the police arrived, Carole had showered and changed and looked more like her usual calm self. Carole had told them what had happened over the phone, but they wanted more details and asked her for a formal statement.

'A car was reported stolen from that car park only a few minutes after you phoned,' the sergeant said, consulting his notebook. 'A blue Ford Orion. Would that be the one?'

'I've no idea,' Carole admitted. 'It was dark. The car didn't have any lights on at first. It was nearly on top of us by the time the lights were switched on, and by then we only had time to dive for cover.'

The sergeant nodded. 'Whoever stole the car probably intended driving out without lights so he wouldn't be seen. Then suddenly he saw your shadows, and had to switch them on to avoid you.'

'But, officer,' Carole said, 'he wasn't trying to avoid us. He seemed to be trying to run us down.'

'Panicked, I expect. Thought he had the car park to himself. Or themselves. Did you see how many people were in the car?'

Carole shook her head. 'Did you, girls?'

'There was a blue car outside the house before we left,' Holly said. 'It followed us into town.'

The sergeant looked interested. 'Followed you into town, you say? And this was the same car?'

Holly bit her lip. Why hadn't she taken more notice? 'I don't know,' she admitted. 'We were in a hurry. I didn't notice the make or the registration number.'

The look of interest faded. He turned back to

130

Carole. 'Is there anything else you can tell me about the incident, Miss Earnshaw?'

'No. Not about this particular incident, but I would like to report something else. Thomas and Ian Clough, who own the Grange at Fram Bight, have put warning notices up all round their land. They say they were put up by the Ministry of Defence, but they're not. There is no Ministry of Defence land around this area.'

The sergeant closed his notebook and a bored expression came over his face. 'We'll look into it.' Then he suddenly became alert again. 'Who did you say, Miss?'

'Thomas and Ian Clough.'

He frowned. 'Funny. It was Mr Ian Clough's car that was stolen from the car park. Could be just a coincidence, but we'll follow it up. Good evening, Miss Earnshaw.' Nodding to the girls, he and the woman police officer went into the hall and Carole showed them out.

Holly couldn't get to sleep for ages. There were too many ideas floating round in her mind. She was convinced that the blue car she had seen outside and the blue Orion in the car park were one and the same. The fact that Ian Clough had reported his car as stolen was a red herring – something to put the police off the scent. But who had been driving it? Not the Spaniard this time. He was still in the restaurant. Not Ian or Thomas either. That left Martyn Hare and Scarface. It could have been either of them or someone else entirely.

It was after midnight and she was still awake. She drew back the curtains. Pulling on her towelling robe, she stood with her elbows on the window-sill, looking out over Framley Bay.

The moon had risen now, a soft yellow harvest moon blurring the outlines of trees and hedges, merging sea and sky and casting a faint mist over the garden. Holly felt relaxed. Next week they'd be back in Willow Vale. Their holiday was going so fast.

Perhaps they'd go swimming tomorrow. It looked as though it was going to be a nice day. They could go down to the cove. It would be an ideal spot for swimming if the tide was right.

Holly yawned. She was about to turn away and go back to bed when a slight movement in the garden caught her eye. A dark shadow separated itself from the bushes by the gate and crept towards the house.

Holly's breath caught in her throat. There was the unmistakeable clatter of the letterbox, then silence. Holly froze. Again she saw the bushes stir, then the shadow was gone and in a few seconds she heard the distant purr of an engine. Then that too was gone.

She waited. The house was as silent as before.

Softly she tiptoed downstairs. A white envelope gleamed on the doormat. Picking it up, she turned it over. There was no name. There was no need for a name. As she opened the envelope, she knew exactly for whom it was meant . . .

THAT WAS JUST A START. YOU'RE NEXT.

11 A stranger at the farm

Holly had no idea what time she eventually fell asleep. But even so, she was up before Tracy and watching the bay through the binoculars.

'You're up early,' Tracy said, pulling on her tracksuit as Holly wandered into the bedroom.

Holly put the note down in front of her. 'The Dutch boat is in the bay again. Anchored. The same as before.'

'How do you know it's the same?' Tracy's eyes danced with excitement.

'I saw the name. *Van Dijk*. They dropped something overboard. It was big and rectangular, like a coffin. They left a buoy marking the spot.' Holly grinned to soften the words.

Tracy shuddered. 'You don't really think it was a coffin do you?'

Holly sighed, her face suddenly serious. 'I suppose not. I was half kidding, I'll admit. But it was the same shape. And it looked heavy. Read the note.'

Tracy read it with a worried frown. 'Are you sure you want to go on with this, Holly?'

'Look. If you want out, that's OK. But you know me. Once I've started I won't stop till it's all wrapped up.'

Tracy spread her hands in a gesture of helplessness. 'If that's the way you want it.'

'Will you do me a favour?' Holly asked. 'This morning do your run up to the Bight instead of the harbour.'

'OK. Do you want me to look out for anything special?'

'Anything. Everything. Something different from the last time we were there.'

Tracy set off, running at her usual easy pace. The morning was clear and fresh, ideal for a run. In spite of the note, and her worry about the danger they were in, she felt good. These early morning runs at Framley were terrific. Better than at home in Willow Vale. There, she was padding along pavements most of the time. Here, she was running on springy turf with the refreshing salty smell of the sea.

She jogged past the Grange, and nearly jumped out of her skin as the Alsatian hurled itself at the gate with a wild bark. 'Hi, Prince,' she said. 'Doing your guard dog act, are you?'

Wetherby's Farm was in the middle of its daily routine. She could hear the noisy mooing of cows, and a dog was trotting through the yard in a business-like manner. A woman in wellies and

135

trousers strode past the gate with a bucket in each hand.

This must be Mrs Wetherby, Tracy thought. It was the same woman they had seen earlier in the week, driving her cows. She'd better make contact. 'Hi,' Tracy said, coming to a stop.

The woman looked startled. 'Who are you?' she said gruffly. 'We don't often see people around at this time in the morning.'

Tracy blinked. What a greeting! Who ever said country people were friendly and soft-hearted?

She tried again. 'I'm staying with Carole Earnshaw, the estate agent.'

'Who?'

Strange woman, Tracy thought. *She can't even remember her own estate agent.* 'Gotta go,' she said, starting to run again. 'See you.'

She ran on down the road and across the sand-dunes on to the beach. The tide was out, and though the thin stretch of sand above the high-water mark was dry and golden, it soon gave way to brown, wrinkled mud where the sea had washed it. She continued running down the beach until she rounded the point that led to the cove. Then she skidded to a halt.

The place was festooned with red-and-white plastic ribbons, like the ones the police use to keep the public away from the scene of a crime. A roughly painted notice hung from a ribbon:

136

KEEP OUT
DANGER OF FALLING ROCKS
BY ORDER

Tracy was puzzled. There had been no notice there before. And there was no sign of fallen rocks. What was going on here? She sat down on a flat rock, looking at the web of plastic tape. Gradually she began to piece it together.

Martyn Hare had said that Thomas Clough was getting suspicious and they would have to move the stuff that night. Last night. Yet Ian and Thomas were eating at the restaurant together. Could it be to keep Thomas out of the way whilst the stuff was being moved? If so, maybe the Spaniard came into the restaurant as a signal that the move was completed. Yes. That was it. And Tracy could make a good guess as to where the stuff had been moved.

The cove. That was why it was sealed off. They'd have to be sure no one went in.

Wait till I tell the others, she thought, grinning with delight.

Then her mood evaporated. The plastic could easily be cut if anyone was determined enough. What would happen if someone got over it and went into the tunnel? Would there be someone on guard to make sure they didn't come out again? A shiver of fear ran up her spine. She was scared, but she just had to find out.

But before she had time to put her theory to the test, Ian Clough walked round the point – the big Alsatian with him.

The dog began to run towards her.

'Prince!' Ian shouted. Obediently it sat down on its haunches.

Ian turned his attention to Tracy. 'Can't you read?' he said roughly.

Hiding her fear, Tracy looked him straight in the eyes. 'It wasn't there before. We were in there a few days ago. There was no sign of a fall then.'

'Do you think the cliff gives you warning before it goes?' Ian asked sarcastically.

He had a point there. 'I'm outside the plastic tape,' she said stubbornly. 'There's nothing to say I can't sit here.'

'*I'm* saying you can't sit here,' he told her. 'So get going before Prince says so too.' There was a threat in his voice beyond the words, and Tracy's stomach did a belly-flop.

She could run fast, but not as fast as an Alsatian. She'd better back down while she had the chance.

'All right, I'm going,' she said, with as much dignity as she could manage. 'Now will you call your dog off?'

'Prince. Stay.'

Tracy got up and walked past the dog back up to the road. Then she began to run, and she didn't stop till she turned into Carole's driveway.

Wait till I tell them, she thought.

But Holly and Belinda had their own news to tell. 'Guess what we've seen?' Holly said excitedly. 'A powerboat came out from the island, went across to the buoy and hauled up the stuff that the Dutch boat dropped.'

Tracy shrugged, feeling deflated. 'Thanks a lot, you guys. You send me off on some wild run to the Bight and then you're so full of your news you don't even want to hear mine.'

'I'm sorry,' Holly said. 'I didn't think. Breakfast's nearly ready. Hot croissants. We'll swap stories while we're eating.'

'Great. I'm starving. How's Carole this morning?'

'Stiff. Lots of bruises. But she's OK. She insisted on going to work.'

After breakfast Tracy got her thoughts together. She told the others what she had worked out about Ian and Thomas and the Spaniard at the Chinese restaurant. 'My guess is, they've moved the stuff to the cove,' she said.

'Brilliant,' Holly said, busily writing it down in the Mystery Club notebook. 'And I told you what we saw. Well, Belinda thinks that the yacht drops the cannabis or whatever it is off the island, and marks it with a buoy. Obviously, a yacht couldn't actually land it on the island. The water is too shallow . . .'

Belinda took over the story, 'Then when the

coast is clear the powerboat delivers it to the mainland.'

Holly finished what she was writing, closed the notebook and with a sigh of satisfaction tucked the pen inside. 'Problem solved,' she said. 'All we want now is the proof. Then we can go to the police.'

'Hang on a minute,' Tracy said. 'There's a slight complication – Mrs Wetherby.'

Holly looked puzzled. 'How is Mrs Wetherby a complication? We haven't even met her yet. What's she got to do with all this?'

Tracy told her about the woman she had met at the farm. 'The same one we saw herding the cows,' she said. 'When I told her I was staying with Carole she didn't know who I was talking about. At the time I thought she was crazy or something. Now I'm beginning to wonder. How did Ian Clough know I was there? Did somebody warn him?' She paused. 'Somebody like Mrs Wetherby, maybe?'

Holly opened the red notebook again. *Mrs Wetherby*, she wrote, and put a big question mark after the name.

Just then the telephone's discreet *Brr . . . Brr* interrupted their conversation. They froze. *Brr . . . Brr*.

'Don't answer it,' Tracy said.

Brr . . . Brr.

'It might be Carole,' Holly said.

Brr . . . Brr.

140

'I'll answer it.' Belinda went into the hall and picked up the phone. She deepened the pitch of her voice and put on a posh accent. 'Carole Earnshaw's residence.'

Sounding startled, a woman's voice said, 'Is that you, Holly? What's wrong with your voice?'

Speaking normally now, Belinda explained that she was trying to sound like a butler.

Carole hooted with laughter. 'I thought you had the most awful cold. Where's that niece of mine?'

'I'll get her.'

When Holly came to the phone Carole explained that she had to see a client in Birmingham. 'It may be after midnight by the time I get home,' she said.

'That's OK,' Holly assured her. 'Don't worry. How's your knee? Are you still stiff?'

'Getting better by the hour.'

'Take care,' Holly said. Then an idea struck her. 'Tracy went past the farm on her run this morning. There was a woman there, but she didn't think it was Mrs Wetherby. What does Mrs Wetherby look like?'

'It must have been her. As far as I know she only has one farm-hand who comes in each day. It's only a small place, and she does a lot of it herself.'

'But what does she look like?' Holly persisted, ready to jot down the description on a piece of paper.

141

'In her sixties. Thin. Weather-beaten kind of face. Grey hair. And you can't miss her eyes. They are the bluest eyes I've ever seen. She's short – about five foot three, but very determined with it. That the one?'

'I guess so. We'd like to go and see her. Do you think she'd mind showing us round? I've never been on a farm.'

'Fine. That should keep you out of mischief whilst I'm away. Tell her you're my niece. But don't make yourself a nuisance. Now I have to go. It's going to be a long day. Make sure you lock all the doors and windows before you go to bed.'

When her aunt had rung off, Holly went back into the kitchen. 'How old would you say that Wetherby woman was?' she asked Tracy. 'What did she look like?'

'Fiftyish. Small. Thin.'

'Could she be sixty?'

Tracy pursed her lips. 'Could be, I suppose. But I doubt it.'

'What colour hair?'

Tracy thought for a moment. 'Difficult to say. It was tucked under a man's cap. Brownish, I think.'

'Eyes?'

'Two.' Tracy grinned.

Holly laughed. 'You mutt. What colour?'

'I didn't really notice. I only exchanged a few words with her.'

'Hmm . . .' Holly looked at her two lists, side by side. 'Could be her. Most likely not. Younger. Different coloured hair. Eyes? We don't know. It's time we went to have a look at Wetherby's Farm. I've cleared it with Carole.'

'Won't the woman think it's a bit odd if I turn up again after being there this morning?' Tracy objected.

'But that's where we're clever,' Holly said mysteriously. 'You're not going to call round. I've got another job for you.'

'It's just as well Carole isn't coming home till late tonight,' Holly said as the three friends cycled towards the Bight. 'That leaves us free to get on with what we have to do. You have the camera, Tracy. It's a new film. Thirty-six exposures, and I've got new batteries in the flash too. Take any photographs you think may be useful for the police. And whatever you do, keep out of sight. OK?'

Tracy looked doubtful. 'Are you sure they'll be bringing the stuff over tonight?'

'Certain. The timetable in the hut showed tonight as the last high tide this month. It's got to be tonight, or why would they mark it? If we're lucky, we'll catch the whole gang in one haul.'

'I wish I had Meltdown with me,' Belinda wailed. 'A horse is more intelligent than a bike. I could whistle for Meltdown and he'd find me somehow.'

'I'm afraid Willow Vale is a bit too far for him to come running today,' Tracy said dryly. 'You'll have to make do with the bike.'

When they got to the Grange Holly said, 'You peel off here, Tracy. Make sure you hide the bike securely. But don't forget where you put it!'

'I won't. See you later.'

Holly and Belinda cycled on. As they neared the farm, the smell of the sea mingled with the fresh smell of manure and other farmyard smells. Holly was looking forward to being shown around.

We'll have to find out who this other woman is, she thought. But she knew they mustn't jump to conclusions. There might be a perfectly normal explanation. Maybe Mrs Wetherby didn't fancy living all on her own on the farm. And who could blame her?

'You do the talking,' she told Belinda. 'It'll give me a better chance to look around for clues and watch her reactions if I'm not actually having to think what to say.'

There was no point in hiding the bikes. It had to look as if they were ordinary visitors who wanted to look at the farm. So they leaned them up against the wall of the cottage and walked up to the front door.

The woman who opened it looked like a typical farmer's wife – tough and wiry. Small and thin, as both Tracy and Carole had said, and her eyes were blue. *She must be the right one*, thought Holly. But Holly would hardly have said they were the bluest eyes she had ever seen. They looked a bit washed out to her.

'Hello,' Belinda said. 'Could I see Mrs Wetherby?'

The woman nodded her head curtly. 'Yes? What do you want?'

'We'd like to look around. We've come from the estate agent.'

Holly drew her breath in sharply. That wasn't the right way to put it at all. She tried to attract Belinda's attention, but she was well away. 'We won't make a nuisance of ourselves, I promise.'

The woman seemed taken aback. 'Bit young, aren't you? Still, the estate agent, you say? Must be all right. Come on in.'

They stepped inside and she closed the door behind them. They were standing in an old-fashioned living-room, with a fire burning in the grate and a mantelpiece covered with pictures and ornaments. Above it was a large mirror, slightly spotted now, but with a beautiful carved gilt frame. The table, the chairs and the sofa were old, but they had been lovingly polished and the atmosphere was cosy.

'I'll get Frank,' the woman said.

Frank? The name rang a bell somewhere.

'Who's Frank?' Holly whispered to Belinda when the woman left the room. 'And why did you

145

say we were from the estate agent? Why not Carole?'

Belinda bit her lip. 'I had a feeling we'd find out more if she didn't know we were connected with Carole.'

When the door from the kitchen was suddenly flung open she remembered immediately where she had heard the name Frank before. The man who stood before them had a long scar running down one side of his face.

12 A startling discovery

Tracy left the others to get on with what they had
to do. She had to get proof of what was going on.
And that meant clear photographs of anything that
might be important.

Where to put the bike? That was the first thing.
It could be vital. If anyone discovered her, she
had to be able to get to the bike in double-quick
time, and get away. She intended to start with
the Clough brothers' vehicles, so she wanted to
dump the bike outside the fence, looking towards
the garages.

On a direct line from the corner post was a clump
of bushes beneath two silver birch trees that grew
so close together they almost made a figure V. She
tucked the bike between the two trunks and stood
back to see how well it was concealed. Yes, that
would do nicely. You'd never notice unless you
knew it was there.

She went back to the fence surrounding the
Grange. On tiptoe she could just see over. Her
eyes raked the house and grounds. There was no

sign of the Alsatian, nor either of the brothers. Not yet, anyway.

Beyond the house was the area where all the vehicles were parked. To the left of the garage she saw the pick-up truck with the searchlight on top of the driver's cab, and a small trailer covered with a tarpaulin.

She turned her attention to the garage. The nose of a blue Orion car with tinted windows stuck out from the ramshackle building. Tracy did a double-take. Wasn't that the car that Ian had reported stolen? The one that had nearly knocked them down? Yet here it was, back in the garage. She smiled to herself. The police might find that rather interesting. She had to get a picture. *Make sure the number plate is clearly visible*, she reminded herself.

Alongside was the white Land Rover. It was definitely the one they had seen outside Martyn Hare's office. She had memorised the number. There was another car, and a van, but they weren't important. No point in wasting exposures and then being short of them later on.

Somehow she had to get down there to examine the Land Rover properly, and to take some close-up pictures. But it wouldn't be wise to climb over the fence here. There was too much open space to cross. What if the dog came at her? She wouldn't have a chance. No, it would be better to work her way round the outside of the fence and get over behind the garages.

She followed the fence deeper into the wood until it turned to run parallel with the cliff. The warning notices that they had seen that first day were still there, but someone had slapped a coat of white paint over the line that said it was by order of the Ministry of Defence. She took a photograph of one of them. It might be useful.

She passed the spot where they had started the climb down to the cove and took a picture of that too.

There was no sign of plastic tape. Perhaps it was further down, at the entrance to the tunnel? *I'll climb down and look at that later*, she thought. A bubble of excitement began to form inside her stomach. When the others had decided she'd better not come with them to the farm, Tracy had been disappointed. She felt as if she were missing all the action. But now, she could feel the excitement taking over.

The fence turned away from the cliff, and she followed it for some distance before peeping over to see where she was. A quick glance told her that this would be as good a place as any. But it was awfully close to the house. She would be visible to anyone who happened to look out of the window. There was a big oak tree whose branches spread well into the grounds. It would be a piece of cake climbing up, whether from this side or to get back out again.

OK, she thought. *Here goes.* Tucking the camera well into the pocket of her anorak, she dug her toes into the massive gnarled trunk and started to climb.

Within a matter of minutes she was sitting astride one of the branches. She looked anxiously at the house. There was no sign or sound that anyone had noticed her, so she dropped quietly over. From there it was only a few yards to the shadowed safety of the garage.

It was the Land Rover she was most interested in. She examined the wing on the driver's side. The paint here was a slightly different colour and as she ran her fingers over the metal she could feel a roughness . . . minute bubbles and dents that weren't visible to the naked eye. She took three exposures – one showing the registration number, the other two close-ups of the wing. She wasn't sure whether the different colour or the surface would show but at least she had it on record.

She moved on to the Orion, standing a few yards away to concentrate on getting a clear, close shot. It had to be right first time. She didn't want to waste another bit of film.

When the voice came, practically in her ear, she jumped so much that she clicked the shutter by reflex. Whirling around, she saw Thomas Clough standing behind her, his face a mixture of disbelief and frustration.

'Don't you lot ever give up? What is it now?'

Tracy's mind went blank. She could only gulp, her heart thudding so loudly in her chest that she thought he must surely hear it.

'Well? I've been watching you for about ten minutes, wondering what on earth you are up to. And I still don't know. What exactly are you doing? And I want a truthful answer.'

He stood, arms folded, as if he were determined to get the truth out of her if it took all day. But somehow it wasn't threatening. She didn't have that sense of fear that she had felt when confronted by his brother earlier on. He wasn't as powerfully built as his brother, but it wasn't that. There was a gentleness about him. A kind of honesty that his brother didn't have.

'I'm taking pictures,' she said weakly.

'I can see that. Why?'

She decided to tell him the truth. 'We – that is, Holly and Belinda and I – think that both these cars were involved in trying to kill us.'

To her surprise, he tilted his head back and roared with laughter. 'Kill you?' he spluttered. 'Why would anyone want to kill you?'

Tracy straightened up defiantly. 'Holly's had two threatening letters. And a phone call,' she added.

Thomas tried to keep his face straight. 'Have you reported it to the police?' he asked.

'Not that,' she admitted. 'But we have told them about the two near-accidents. One with this . . .' She pointed to the Land Rover. 'And the other with this.' She stood with her hand on the bonnet of the Orion. 'Tell me, Mr Clough, why is this car here in your garage when your brother reported it stolen last night?'

A gleam of amusement lit his dark eyes. 'Because, my dear detective, the police found it abandoned about eight miles the other side of Framley at two o'clock this morning. Satisfied?'

Tracy's confident mood evaporated. 'There's still the other one,' she blustered. 'This *is* your brother's Land Rover, isn't it?'

'Actually,' he said dryly, 'it's registered in my name, but, yes . . . my brother drives it. Why?'

'When Carole was taking us home from the Grange the other day a white Land Rover drove us off the road.'

Thomas looked surprised and a little uneasy. 'I didn't know. But why do you think it was my Land Rover?'

She swung round to put her hand on the driver's wing. 'Feel this,' she said. 'You can still feel the nicks and bumps where it's been repaired.' She bent down to look along the surface. 'You can see by the paintwork, too. You look.'

He considered her for a moment before replying. 'I don't need to look. Your detective work on this occasion is spot on. We had the wing repaired the following day. But I assure you that the story I heard had nothing to do with driving you – or anyone else – off the road. I'll have a word with my brother. Now, anything else?'

Tracy took a deep breath. There would never be another chance like this. Thomas was actually smiling at her.

'Did you know that your brother was involved with drugs?'

His face darkened. For a moment she thought he was going to hit her, and she took a step back.

'I don't know how you heard about that,' he growled. 'It was years ago, when he was at college. He and Martyn Hare got in some silly scrape. But that's over. Done. Believe me.'

Tracy couldn't take it all in. So Ian Clough and Martyn Hare were at college together. That explained a lot. *Wait till I tell the others*, she thought.

Yet she felt sorry for Thomas. He obviously believed in his brother. It made her feel embarrassed at bringing it up. But how was she to know that Thomas would think she was referring to something that happened ages ago?

'I've got to go,' she said. 'Belinda and Holly will be waiting for me.'

Thomas walked with her to the gate. She didn't tell him that she'd left her bike in the woods and got over the fence via a tree. She would have felt a bit silly climbing up a branch with him watching. The gate seemed the sensible option.

As she walked on down the road she puzzled over what she had heard. And there was the business about the cars too. She still wasn't sure about the Orion. It was the car all right, but maybe Ian didn't have anything to do with the incident after all. But the Land Rover! That was well and truly a success. They could clear that bit up in the Mystery Club notebook anyway.

The cove was next. That's where they had arranged to meet. She wondered how the others had got on at the farm. If their bikes were still outside then they were still there. If not, they had gone on to the cove and would see her on the cliff top.

Their bikes were gone from the farm. But Holly and Belinda weren't at the cliff top.

She wandered up and down for a while, calling their names. A breeze was blowing up and Tracy began to feel chilly. Should she go down into the cove now and take some photographs, or should she wait for them a while longer?

She didn't feel like going down to the cove on her own. She might meet Ian Clough and she didn't fancy that – especially if Thomas had already spoken to him about running them into the hedge. He wouldn't be too pleased about that.

She went back to the farm and knocked at the door. The woman she had seen before opened it.

'Hi, remember me?' Tracy said in her friendliest voice. 'I saw you this morning when I was on my run.'

The woman grunted a reluctant, 'Yes.'

'My friends were hoping to have a look round the farm. Have they been yet? They said they'd meet me at the Bight.'

The woman shook her head. 'Haven't seen 'em. Anyway, I wouldn't show 'em round. What d'you think this is – the National Trust?' She closed the door.

Tracy felt as if she had been slapped. She turned to go, but stopped in her tracks. A bright square of red caught her attention. *That's odd*, she thought.

She took a closer look. Half hidden in the flower border, there it was – the Mystery Club notebook!

So they *had* been here. The woman was lying.

Carefully casual, Tracy slipped the notebook under her T-shirt. She strolled through the garden gate and back on to the road. Her feet automatically turned towards the beach, her mind churning.

As she passed the farmyard she saw a slight movement out of the corner of her eye. A man started to come out of one of the sheds, then stepped back into the shadows. It was only a brief glimpse, but enough to be able to tell that he had a scar running right down one side of his face.

Tracy walked on as if she hadn't noticed anything, but now her mind was working furiously. What was Scarface doing at the farm? Had he recognised her? She bit her lip, trying to work out what had happened to Holly and Belinda. Had they seen Scarface and decided to do some crafty detective work? Or had they fallen into a trap?

Holly would never have given up that notebook willingly, she thought. She wouldn't just drop it either. So they must have been trapped. With a shudder, she remembered the note. THAT WAS JUST A START. YOU'RE NEXT.

It's up to me now, she thought. *And I'd better be quick.*

When she got to the end of the road, where it became scrubby grass and low sand-dunes, Tracy turned right towards the jetty. Then she doubled back again, dodging through bushes, skirting hedgerows, always looking back over her shoulder to see if anyone was following. But no one did. Perhaps they thought they had convinced her. And they would have . . . except for the red notebook.

At last she was back at the farm. There wasn't as much cover here as at the Grange. But it was enough. Just. There were no walls or fences around this place – only three strands of barbed-wire on posts strung around the farmyard and cottage,

156

and a double-width metal gate leading out into the pasture. There was nothing to hide behind, but on the other hand there was nothing to have to climb over. She could easily slip between those strands.

She counted the various outbuildings. There were two big barns, one long single-storey building that she guessed was the milking shed and a couple of smaller sheds that could be anything. Five in total. Then there was the house. Maybe they were in the house? But there were at least two people there she would have to dodge.

Still, she had to do something. Holly and Belinda would be relying on her to come up with something. She clenched her fists.

Hang in there, guys, she said silently. *I'm on my way . . .*

13 Trapped!

When Scarface came into the living-room of the Wetherby farmhouse and saw Belinda and Holly, his mouth stretched into what should have been a smile. 'I had a funny feeling you'd eventually end up here,' he said. 'And I do mean "end up".' The meaning was only too clear.

'You've met Mrs Wetherby,' he said, indicating the woman who stood by the door. 'Unfortunately for you, when you said you'd come from the estate agent she thought you meant Bingley and Hare.'

'She's not Mrs Wetherby,' Holly said scornfully, 'or she'd have known that my aunt had taken over the sale of the farm.'

'No,' he admitted, 'she's not. But she'll do very well for the time being. "Mrs Wetherby, Mark Two", you might say.' He gave a little snort of laughter at his own joke.

'How long do you think you're going to be able to keep this up?' Holly demanded.

'For as long as I need. Mrs Wetherby is going to sell the farm to us. And at a very satisfactory

158

price . . .' He paused. 'Satisfactory for us, that is. Yes, I thought that would surprise you. Martyn Hare has drawn up the contract. Only it will be this Mrs Wetherby who'll be doing the signing.'

'And what about when the real Mrs Wetherby finds out what you've done?' Holly asked.

He shrugged. 'She's in such a confused state, she won't know what she's signed or what she hasn't signed.'

Holly tried to bluff it out. 'OK. You win,' she said. 'Come on, Belinda.'

'Oh, no you don't,' Scarface said. As swiftly as a snake he had crossed the room and was barring their exit with a knife.

The girls froze.

'That's better,' he said.

He turned to the woman. 'Get some rope and tie them up.'

She went out, and Scarface slumped down on the arm of a chair by the door, one boot casually propped up on the upholstery. He cleaned under his fingernails with the knife, wiping the dirt on his trousers.

Holly tried to think of a way to escape. *We should have been more careful after what Tracy said*, she said to herself. *Tracy!* There was always Tracy. She was probably looking for them already. She would see the bikes and know they were there. As long as she didn't walk into the trap too . . .

Holly gave Belinda a questioning look. 'Tracy,' she mouthed silently. Belinda glanced at Scarface, who was still engrossed in his nails. She nodded and crossed her fingers.

The woman came back with a length of rope. Expertly, she bound their hands and legs and soon the girls were trussed and gagged, completely unable to move.

'Get their bikes,' he ordered. 'Put them in the cowshed for now.'

'What are we going to do with them?' she asked, nodding towards the girls.

'The attic I think, for today. And tomorrow perhaps a little trip in the boat.' He laughed. 'They won't be the first swimming accident on this coast.'

Holly's throat went dry. The gag bit into the corners of her mouth and she felt as if she were choking. They were going to be killed!

Through the window Holly could see the woman wheeling the two bikes away from the garden and into the farmyard. One fell into the flower-beds and she heard a loud curse. Then the woman was out of sight and so were the bikes.

Holly's heart sank. Without the bikes how would Tracy know they were here? Or even that they had been there at all? There must be a way. But what?

When she came back, they were pushed and prodded up the stairs and along a narrow corridor with doors on either side. *Bedrooms*, Holly thought, trying to keep a sense of direction. She had to remember which was the front and which the back. This could make the difference between escape and death.

As they were passing one door, a weak voice called, 'Frank? Is that you, Frank?'

Scarface gripped Holly tightly, holding the knife to her throat.

'I'll be with you in a minute, Mrs Wetherby.'

So that was where the real Mrs Wetherby was, Holly thought. There was a light in the corridor opposite her door. *Remember that*, she told herself.

Then she and Belinda were once more propelled forward, up a short wooden staircase. Scarface thrust them into a room with sloping ceilings and a distinct smell of damp.

'You look after the kids,' he commanded, pushing Belinda and Holly towards the woman. 'I'll see what the old bag wants.' Then he vanished, closing the door after him.

The room was a jumble of relics from long ago – a rocking horse, a couple of wooden cupboards, toys, a pile of books and magazines and a rusty brass chest.

At the far end was a wing chair, the stuffing sticking out of the arms, and a bed, the mattress sagging almost to the floor. It had obviously been a servant's bedroom at one time –

many years ago. There was even a washstand and jug.

Holly had an idea. She began wriggling, making noises as if she wanted to attract the woman's attention.

'Quiet,' the woman said.

But Holly continued more vigorously this time.

The woman came over and loosened her gag. 'What is it?'

'I need to go to the loo,' Holly said. It was worth a try. At least it would give her another chance to get to know her way around.

'Too bad.'

'I *need* to,' she said, putting a note of desperation in her voice.

The woman hesitated. 'You'll have to wait till Frank gets back.'

'Will he be long?'

The woman suddenly lost patience. 'Shut up and wait,' she said. Savagely she retied the gag, pulling it even tighter.

In the distance she heard a telephone ring. The woman was listening too, as if it was the signal they had been waiting for.

When Scarface came back he was in a bad mood. 'That was Martyn Hare,' he said. 'Old Bingley insists on coming with him for the signing of the contract tomorrow. He knows the old woman. That means we can't use you after all. Not to sign,

162

anyway. Still, you'll make a useful back-up. A respectable married couple buying a farm for their old age, eh?' He gave a short laugh, as if the idea amused him.

'What if he says she's round the bend?'

He shook his head. 'He won't. I'll only give her half the dose tomorrow. She'll be nicely relaxed and sleepy, but she won't have a clue what's going on. She trusts me. Said she didn't know what she'd do without me. She believes every word I say. When I told her that the vet said the sheep died from anthrax brought over from the island she insisted on writing a letter to the Ministry of Defence.' He snorted his contempt. 'I tore it up.'

Holly wriggled and gave a muffled cry.

The woman nodded towards her. 'She wants to use the loo,' she told him.

'Well, she can't,' he snarled.

Holly wriggled some more.

Scarface stared at her through narrowed eyes. Then, as if he had decided she was totally within his power, he gave a nod. 'OK. Take her to the bathroom. But don't try anything stupid,' he said, glaring at Holly.

She rolled her eyes, shaking her head.

When they got to the bathroom, Holly motioned to her gag again. Impatiently, the woman released it.

'Now what?'

'I need my hands free.'

With a sour expression on her face, the woman untied Holly's wrists. 'Don't be too long. I'll wait outside.'

Holly had been hoping she'd say that. Luckily, the bathroom door had been open as they were being taken upstairs and she had realised that it faced the front of the house. It was only a chance, but better than nothing. Feverishly, she tried to loosen the ropes round her legs. Loosen them, she thought – not untie. Or else the woman would tie them up even tighter and there'd never be another chance.

In her hurry, she was almost sobbing. Why wouldn't the knots give? *Come on*, she urged silently.

'Are you ready?'

Struggling to keep her voice steady, Holly called, 'Nearly.'

With relief she felt one of the knots give, and she was able to move her legs slightly. That would have to do for now. She took the Mystery Club notebook and a pen out of her jacket and scribbled a note:

SCARFACE IS HERE.
WE ARE PRISONERS IN ATTIC.
GET HELP.
HOLLY.

'Haven't you finished yet?' The voice was muffled by the door.

'Almost.' Quietly, she eased the sash window down to halfway and tossed the notebook out as far as she could. It flapped downwards like a bright red bird. *Please let Tracy see it before anyone else*, she prayed, opening the door.

Meekly, Holly held her wrists out in front of her. The woman automatically tied them together, not realising that earlier they had been tied behind her back. Holly eased her wrists slightly apart as the woman pulled at the knots, dropping her hands well down in the hope that Scarface wouldn't notice the change. Then she hobbled after the woman as if her legs were as tightly bound as before.

Back in the room, Scarface was scowling impatiently. 'Right,' he said. 'I've fixed the fat one. Tie them together, back to back. Then come down and give me a hand. We've got about forty-five minutes before Martyn Hare arrives. Make sure you lock the door, just in case.'

The woman nodded, and Scarface left. They heard his footsteps going down the uncarpeted stairs to the first floor, then silence. The woman roughly pushed her on to the bed alongside Belinda, and bent down to tie them together. Holly gave a little cry and the woman loosened the bonds slightly.

I should be an actress, Holly said to herself.

As soon as they were alone Holly twisted her wrists to and fro, trying to ease the bonds that were holding them. But they wouldn't budge. The rope cut into her skin, making it red and swollen. She relaxed, giving the swelling a moment to subside, then she scrunched her hands together and with a sudden twist yanked them loose.

It was as much as she could do not to yell out with the pain. But there was no time to think of that now. In spite of her bleeding hands she pulled frantically at the knots that were still holding her ankles. Then it was the turn of the gag, and at last she was free.

By the time she had freed Belinda too, a precious twenty minutes had gone by. Belinda rubbed at her wrists and ankles. 'The fat one!' she said indignantly. 'He called me the fat one.' She looked at Holly and grinned. 'I guess that next to you I am.'

'I've been looking at the walls,' Holly said. 'They're very thin. Just plywood panels nailed together. I reckon we ought to be able to prise one of them away and see what's behind.'

The two girls went round the room testing for loose panels. But they were tougher than they looked. Panel after panel refused to move. They had almost given up, when at last Holly felt one give.

'Belinda! Over here,' she whispered.

After a lot of tugging and broken and splintered nails they managed to pull it away from its neighbour. Stepping into the darkness beyond, Holly looked back at Belinda. 'You stay there, to cover for me. Prop the board back so it looks OK. If anyone comes, hit them over the head or something.'

'Thanks a lot,' Belinda groaned. 'With friends like you who needs enemies?'

Holly stepped into the space behind the walls and the light was shut out as Belinda put back the board. For a moment she stood, balanced on the thin joists, unable to see a thing. Then, as her eyes became accustomed to the gloom she was able to make out the pattern of wooden joists with a carpet of insulation fibre lying like cotton wool between them. She knew she could only walk on the wood. Otherwise she might go straight through, and land up in the room below.

At first, it seemed almost impossible to balance on the narrow strips of wood, but once she figured out that she could hold on to the beams that supported the roof, she managed to move about quite easily.

It was only when she saw a square of wood cleared of the insulation fibre that she realised there was easy access via a trap-door to each of the upstairs rooms. Warily she eased her fingers beneath the trap-door and lifted it slightly. Two men were talking . . .

'Why do you have to bring old Bingley?'

'He saw the office diary. Once he knew I was coming to see Mrs Wetherby he insisted on being here tomorrow. They must have had quite a thing going between them when they were young. Said he had lost contact with her, but he's obviously keen to see her again.'

That must be Martyn Hare, Holly thought. Bingley was the partner that Carole had told them about. The one who was more or less retired and only came in once or twice a week. Who was the other man talking? she wondered. He didn't sound like Scarface. She wondered if she dared open the trap-door a little further so that she could see who it was.

'Do you think we could still get away with palming the other woman off as Mrs Wetherby? We could warn him that she's changed since her husband died.'

'No. It's not worth chancing. If Bingley rumbles that there's anything fishy going on he could stop me getting my hands on the island, and that would be the end of our drugs run. At the moment he thinks I'm helping him restock the place for his stupid wildlife sanctuary.'

Holly tried to make sense of what she was hearing. She thought back to what she had been told at the coastguards' office. Suddenly, it all began to fit together . . .

Could Bingley be the new owner of the island? If so, that would give Martyn Hare a reason for visiting the place. And if it became a wildlife sanctuary, that would be a good excuse for stopping people landing there. And a perfect cover for the drugs run – especially when they could be hidden at the farm run by yet another of the gang . . .

The second voice chimed in. 'What about Frank? I don't trust him.'

'He's handy for delivering the stuff. Nobody's going to bother to examine a lorry taking animals to market. It's safer than your scrapyard vehicles anyway. Besides, your brother's getting suspicious. You told me that yourself. But if Frank begins to get too big for his boots we'll get rid of him. I can handle the woman all right.'

As soon as the scrapyard was mentioned, Holly knew who was speaking. Ian Clough. Of course!

He spoke again. 'Sounds as if you've got it all sussed out.'

Martyn Hare laughed. 'You bet I have. Do you think I'd have buried myself in this godforsaken town if there was nothing in it for me? My father used to be in partnership with Bingley. That's how I knew the island was to be decontaminated and returned to its original owners. I knew that Bingley was the only surviving heir, so when Dad died I took over the partnership and Dad's share of the deal with the island.'

Ian Clough broke in. 'I'd better get down to the cove. It will be high tide soon. Got to get fixed up for the run. This is the big one.'

'Good. Tell Frank to give old Bingley plenty to drink when he arrives. A couple of large whiskies and he won't look too closely at what he's signing.'

The voices faded, and Holly heard the door close as the two men moved out of the room. She waited a moment to make sure that they weren't coming back, then lifted the trap-door and dropped into the room. It was a bedroom facing the back of the house. Simply furnished, it had been used quite recently. There was a man's jacket over the back of one of the chairs, and a tie slung over the mirror on the old-fashioned dressing-table. Frank's room? It wouldn't be wise to hang around to find out.

Holly slipped out into the corridor. A little further along was the light that she had remembered was outside Mrs Wetherby's room. Now was her chance. She hurried along the corridor, putting her ear to the door to listen before opening it.

A woman was sitting in a tall wing chair, facing the gas-fire. Her back was to the door, her pale face turned towards the window. It was a kind face, framed with greying hair and, as Carole had said, the bluest eyes she'd ever seen. But as Holly looked she heard a gasp and the woman put a hand to her mouth as if to stifle a scream.

She was staring at the window – her eyes wide. And as Holly followed her gaze she saw why . . .

14 Avalanche!

'Tracy!'

Holly ran to the window, pushing up the heavy sash. Then, remembering that with one scream Mrs Wetherby could ruin everything, she turned round and put her finger to her lips. 'Don't call for help, Mrs Wetherby. *Please!*' she implored. 'We're not here to harm you – we're here to help. Give me a minute and I'll explain.'

Mrs Wetherby looked bewildered. She wiped a hand across her forehead, as if to clear her vision. As if she weren't sure whether she was really awake or not.

Holly helped her friend off the ladder and into the room. 'Good old Tracy. Are the police on their way?'

Tracy shook her head. 'I didn't know what to do, or where you were. It was only when I saw the notebook that I guessed you were in trouble. Then when I was looking for a ladder I found your bikes and I *knew* you were in trouble.'

'But you saw my note?'

'What note?'

'In the book. I left a note to tell you to get help.'

When she saw Tracy's puzzled expression, Holly gave a sigh. 'Oh, well, never mind. We'll manage.'

But first they had to find somewhere to hide. Swiftly, Holly went across to the double bed and lifted up the heavy woven bedspread. Yes, there was plenty of room, and the cover hung well down on both sides. No one would see them there.

'Mrs Wetherby,' Holly asked gently, turning to the old woman, 'do you know what's wrong with you?'

The old lady frowned, as if she couldn't quite pull her thoughts together. Then she nodded. 'Arthritis.' She managed a weak smile, 'And old age too, I guess. It's all got beyond me since my husband died. How I'd manage without Frank, I don't know. He brings my pain-killers from the doctor's surgery every month. I can't drive any more. I'm too weak.'

'Mrs Wetherby, I don't believe it's pain-killers that Frank is giving you. I think he's keeping you drugged with tranquillisers. He's persuaded you to sell him the farm, hasn't he?'

Mrs Wetherby closed her eyes wearily. 'Has he? Perhaps he has. I've been trying to sell the farm for ages.' She thought for a minute. 'I had some

173

tranquillisers when my husband died. But I only used them for a couple of days. They should be in the bathroom cabinet.'

'I'll look. Tracy, wait here. If anyone comes get under the bed.'

Holly opened the door and looked up and down the corridor. Nobody there. Silently she sped to the bathroom, and looked in the medicine cabinet. There was a small brown bottle of Valium with three tablets left in the bottom.

'Is this them?' she asked when she got back.

Mrs Wetherby stared at the bottle. 'But I haven't taken all those.'

'You have,' Holly said. 'Only you didn't know it.'

'But why? I don't understand.'

Holly gave her a brief outline of the story. 'So you see,' she concluded, 'the woman you know as Frank's wife is pretending to be you. They're keeping you doped so you don't know how little you are selling it for.'

Holly didn't know quite how much Mrs Wetherby was able to take in, and by the time she finished the old lady was even more pale and drawn than before.

'All this, just to get me to sell him the farm?'

Holly nodded. 'They need a safe place to store the drugs. Martyn Hare and Ian Clough buy the stuff in Holland. From there it's shipped to the island, and from there it has been going to a cove below the cliff. But that's not safe any more. They need the farm to be able to hide it before delivery to the big cities. You're isolated here. You've even got a jetty. This place is perfect for them. They daren't chance you selling it to someone else.'

'What do you want me to do?'

'Can you telephone the police without Scarface – I mean Frank – knowing? Tell them about the drugs and ask them to come immediately. Tracy, get the ladder out of sight as fast as you can, so they won't know you've been here. Then go to the Grange and watch out for Ian Clough.'

Tracy looked anxious. 'OK. But what about Belinda? Where is she?'

'She's still in the attic. I'll go and get her now, then we'll go to the cove and see if we can set a trap to catch them with the drugs.'

Suddenly they heard footsteps coming along the corridor.

'Quick!' Holly gasped. 'Somebody's coming.'

In an instant Tracy was out of the window and climbing down the ladder. Meanwhile Holly scrambled into her hiding-place under the bed. Seconds later, the door opened and as she peered out from under the bedcover Holly saw the ladder sway and disappear from sight. Then a pair of legs walked past the bed and she heard the clatter of a tray.

'Wake up, Mrs Wetherby. I've brought your

supper and your tablets. Eat up while it's nice and hot.' It was a woman's voice. Frank's woman.

As the voice went on, Holly's heart missed a beat. There on the floor, just out of reach, lay the Mystery Club notebook! You couldn't miss it. In an agony of fury, Holly clenched her fists, digging her nails into her hands in sheer frustration. To be caught now, just as she thought they were out of danger.

Perhaps I could rush her, she thought. *Catch her unawares as she bends down to pick it up.*

She waited for the woman to stop beside the book, but miraculously she didn't. The legs changed direction, crossing over towards the window. Holly's breath caught in her throat. Had Tracy got the ladder away in time?

'Aren't you cold, Mrs Wetherby? Shall I close the window?'

The answer came swiftly. 'No. Leave it.'

Holly's heart slowed to a more normal beat. Saved again.

'Anything else, Mrs Wetherby? Shall I help you get into bed? Or shall I come back later?'

'No, thank you. I can manage on my own. You needn't come back for the tray either. I don't want to be disturbed.'

Holly breathed a sigh of relief. It wouldn't do to have the woman coming back unexpectedly.

The legs moved out of her line of vision, and she heard the door close. When she was sure they were alone, Holly wriggled out from her hiding-place. 'Well done, Mrs Wetherby,' she said.

The old woman smiled, and there was a faint sparkle of excitement in her blue eyes. 'It's like being in a detective story,' she said. 'But what shall we do with the tablets she put on my plate? Mustn't leave them there where Frank will see them, or he'll guess I'm on to him.'

Holly grinned. 'You're not such a bad detective yourself.' She bent down to pick up the red notebook. 'Give me the tablets. I'll chuck them out of the window.' She picked them up from the tray, lowered the window slightly and tossed them out. 'I'm off now. Remember, tell the police about the drugs and ask them to come to Fram Bight as quickly as they can.'

After checking that there was no one around, she slipped out of the room and along the corridor to the short wooden stairs that led to the attic. The door at the top of the stairs was closed, but not locked. 'Belinda,' she whispered. 'It's me. Holly!'

'Come on in.'

Cautiously, she pushed open the door, then stopped in amazement. Belinda was kneeling on the floor, tying up the woman who had posed as Mrs Wetherby. The woman was unconscious, lying face down, her eyes closed. And alongside her were the remains of a large blue vase, now smashed beyond repair.

'I hope the vase wasn't valuable,' Belinda joked. 'It's not much use now.'

'I don't think Mrs Wetherby will mind.' Holly grinned. 'I'll give you a hand.'

Together they tied and gagged the woman, while Holly brought her friend up to date with what had been happening. Then they locked and bolted the door, and tiptoed downstairs.

'That shortens the odds,' Belinda whispered. 'Two of us against one of him – even if he has got a knife.'

There was no sign of movement downstairs, and though it was getting dark the lights had not yet been switched on. 'Perhaps he's busy with the animals,' Belinda said. 'After all, he *does* work here.'

Sure enough, when they got outside they could hear the milking machine, and see the lights in the long cowshed. 'We'll have to leave the bikes where they are,' Holly whispered. 'Come on.'

Bending down to keep within the shadow of the wall, the two girls crept past the farmyard and hurried down the road towards the cliffs.

When they had almost reached the shallow strip of marram grass and dunes that marked the beginning of the beach they heard the heavy throb of an engine.

'Dive for cover!' Holly cried, throwing herself into a tangle of brambles.

The tractor chugged noisily past, dragging a small trailer behind it. Driving it was Ian Clough. He looked straight ahead, his jaw set with determination. There was a tension in the way his hands gripped the steering-wheel that reminded Holly of what she had overheard. This was going to be the 'big one'. She knew exactly what that meant. This was going to be the biggest load of drugs they had handled so far. And, she guessed, this was the vehicle they were going to use to transport them from the cove.

Dusk was falling rapidly, and Holly almost missed the dark figure that came cycling along the footpath some way behind the tractor. Tracy! She was concentrating so hard on following the tractor without being seen that she almost fell off the bike when Holly climbed to her feet out of the brambles.

The bike wobbled to a stop. 'Where's Belinda?' Tracy asked, her cheeks red.

'I'm here.' Belinda was lying on her back in a patch of stinging nettles. 'Give me a hand.'

'How on earth did you land up there?' Holly laughed, as she reached down to pull her up.

'Well, I didn't see them, did I?' Belinda said indignantly. 'My glasses fell off, and I thought it was just a pile of tall grasses.'

'Oh, no,' Holly groaned. 'Not again. Don't tell me you've lost them again?'

Belinda nodded miserably.

'We're not going to search around with bare hands in a patch of stinging nettles. You'll have to manage without them for now. Come on.' She dragged Belinda along behind her and the three girls headed for the beach in the wake of the tractor.

Just then the engine cut out. They were taken by surprise, and froze like statues. 'What's happening?' Tracy whispered.

'Shh . . . He might hear us.'

It must be almost high tide, Holly thought. Any minute now the signalling would begin. She tried to work out how many people they would have to deal with. Ian Clough for a start. Scarface? He was still at the farm. The woman was well out of the way, too. Holly giggled at the thought. She was willing to bet that Martyn Hare wouldn't get himself involved in the actual drug-running either. That left the Spaniard. Three girls to two men. No problem. They could manage that all right.

But they needed the police to get the smugglers arrested. Could they rely on Mrs Wetherby being able to phone? What if she didn't?

'Tracy? How long do you think it would take you to get to the police station?'

'On the bike?'

'Of course. How else?'

Tracy blew out her lips in thought. 'Ten minutes . . . fifteen perhaps.'

'Right. Go like the clappers. Get them down here in double-quick time. Tell them the truth, tell them lies: just get them here! And quietly. No sirens wailing. Impress upon them the importance of silence if they want to catch the drugs gang. OK?'

'I'm on my way.' The next second Tracy was on the bike and pedalling away up the road like the wind.

'Just us now, Belinda. Are you OK?'

Belinda's voice had a slight tremble in it, but her answer was positive. 'Of course I'm OK. I can't see properly that's all. Everything's a bit blurred. But once it gets dark we'll all be in the same boat.'

Holly explained her plan. 'First we must find the trailer and uncouple it from the tractor while Ian Clough is fixing up the lights. Come on. I expect it's on the cliff, near the entrance to the cove.'

Cautiously they crept along the path, until they reached the tractor and trailer standing silent and driverless on the cliff top. Holly's heart was beating fast. Would they be able to separate it from the tractor without being seen? More important, would they know how?

She could have jumped for joy when she saw the connecting mechanism. It would be no more difficult than uncoupling a caravan from a car. She'd helped with that dozens of times. It was only a matter of strength . . . lifting the trailer bar off the socket on the back of the tractor. It was a little trailer, so it would be lighter than lifting the towbar of a caravan.

'Come on, Belinda,' she whispered. 'This doesn't need 20/20 vision, just brute strength. Lift this up while I uncouple it.'

Without a sound, the two friends separated the two units, then straightened up – one part of their mission accomplished. But Holly suddenly realised that the trailer was slowly beginning to move down the slope towards the cliffs. Grabbing at the metal bar, she dug her heels in the soft grass. The shock nearly tore her shoulders out of their sockets, but even that did not stop it.

'Belinda!'

Belinda added her weight to Holly's and the trailer ground to a halt. They hung there for a few seconds, their minds shocked into numbness.

Belinda worked it out first. 'Can you see any brakes?'

Holly gritted her teeth. 'No,' she gasped. 'Perhaps it doesn't have a separate brake.'

'I'm heavier than you, so my weight will counterbalance it better. Anyway, you've got better eyesight. I'll hang on here while you find some stones to put under the wheels.'

'Are you sure you can hold it?'

Belinda nodded. 'Go on.'

Bit by bit Holly released her hold. Belinda's heels sunk lower into the ground, but the trailer didn't move.

Desperately, Holly scoured the area. Every stone she picked up was either too small, too light, or too brittle. Would she never find the right ones?

Then at last, there they were, a couple of well rounded, solid pebbles. She didn't know whether they would be heavy enough but they'd have to do. With trembling hands, she pushed them under the wheels and Belinda slowly released her hold.

They stood back – hardly daring to believe that the vehicle wouldn't start rolling down the slope again. But it didn't. They'd done it!

Next, they had to put the light out of action. If Ian Clough had any idea that his plan was in jeopardy he might try to stop the boat coming over from the island. And they had to have the drugs here. That was the evidence. Without it there could be no arrests.

'Come on,' Holly urged. 'I'll guide you.'

Carefully and quietly the two girls worked their way down the zigzag path to the entrance to the tunnel. In the distance they could hear the waves slapping against the rocks in the cove below. Then came a strange noise, amplified in the hollow bowl of rock. A door creaked open on rusty hinges, and Holly heard the unmistakeable clatter of metal being wheeled over concrete.

'The light!' Holly gasped. 'He's wheeling out the light. Wait here. I'll be back.'

Before Belinda had time to answer, Holly was scrambling along the ridge of rock that acted as a roof to the inner part of the cove. The signals from the island had already started. Holly knew it by heart. One white, one green, one white, one red – with pauses in-between. That gave her very little time. Perhaps three or four minutes before he would start his reply.

The shelf of rock had widened now, with a gap between the two sides so that she could look down into the cove itself. She heard the heavy rasp of Ian Clough's breathing as he moved the lamp and generator to a more open space.

Here, previous falls from the cliffs higher up had left a giant's playground of boulders and shale. If she could get one of the bigger boulders moving it might be enough to start a small avalanche. Enough to make Ian Clough move out of range even if it were not enough to put the light out of action.

A few feet higher up the slope one boulder stood poised on its edge. It looked as if it would move in a puff of wind, but when Holly tried to push it over, she realised that it was solidly jammed against a wall of pebbles and stones. Frantically she scrabbled at them, ignoring the pain of scratched and bruised hands . . . aware only of the balancing needs of speed and silence.

Then, when she had almost given up hope, the boulder rocked a little on its perch. Holly's stomach gave a lurch of relief and hope. She leapt round behind it, and rounding her back against its enormous bulk, she pushed with all her might.

When it went, it went with a rush – sending her sprawling. She felt herself falling . . . slithering down the same path as the boulder as if she too would crash into the cove beneath. Panic-stricken, she grabbed at every ledge, every rock within her reach, sending them skittering down the cliff, bouncing and rebounding from rock to rock till their fall echoed like crashes of thunder in the cove below.

15 Clearing up

At last her fingers held, and the mad headlong fall
was halted. She hung there for a long moment,
afraid to move. When she had got her breath back
she felt around for a toe-hold, and gradually –
inch by inch – managed to pull herself back to
safety.

Below her she heard a flood of curses as Ian
Clough picked himself up. He swore at everything:
the unsafe cliffs, the useless light, the darkness,
the drugs . . . nothing escaped his violent temper.
Holly was glad that he had not discovered her part
in the rock-fall.

He was still muttering to himself as she crept
back to join Belinda – her face a pale blur in the
gloom.

'What about that, then?' Holly grinned, gently
brushing the grit from her grazed hands. 'Rather
effective, I thought – even if I almost killed myself
in the process.'

Belinda grinned back. 'I thought you had.'

'Let's get back to the cliff top,' Holly said. 'We

can see more from there. We'll plan our next move as we go.'

A few minutes later, they were kneeling in the bracken, well away from the tractor in case Ian returned. The moon was just rising, cutting a swathe of silver across the water. It all looked so peaceful and serene. But then she saw the dark shape of a boat chugging quietly towards the cove. It was time for action.

'As soon as that boat gets to the cove,' she said, 'we've got to find another way down and put it out of action. You know boats, Belinda. Any idea how to do it?'

'We could cut the fuel pipe. That would stop them.'

'Oh, yes . . . but what with?'

Belinda dug into her pocket and brought out a knife. 'The woman brought this with her when she came up to the attic. When I knocked her out she dropped it. I thought it might come in useful.'

'You're absolutely brilliant, Belinda. Come on, we've got to find another way down the cliff.'

The loaded boat inched its way into the cove as the girls climbed down the cliff. Although the night sky was clear, the moon threw strange shadows over the rocks so that it was difficult to pick out the pathway safely. Belinda followed blindly, as Holly guided her to secure footholds with whispered instructions.

At last they were just a couple of feet above the water. Holly pushed Belinda into a split in the cliff, and told her to wait. Edging carefully round into the entrance to the cove, Holly saw the boat. She could hear voices coming from the tunnel, but there was one crate still to unload – with the strange red and green logo stencilled on the side.

Flattening herself against the wall of rock, she heard the voices come closer.

'It'll be another week before the *Van Dijk* does this run again. No point in your staying over on the island till then. I'll unpack the crates at the farm and Frank can load it up on the cattle truck in the morning.'

'Must I go back to the island tonight? Can't I leave the boat here?' Holly guessed at once who it was. There was no mistaking that Spanish accent.

Clough's reply was rough. 'You'll do as you're told. My brother could come down here at any time. He's suspicious enough as it is. And those kids have been interfering again. I'm going to shut them up for good this time.'

The Spaniard muttered something she didn't quite catch, but Ian Clough's reply was clear enough.

'No problem. I'll come over and fetch you in the morning. As soon as we've loaded the cattle for Sheffield market you'll be on your way. Our contact is expecting you. It's worth a cool million. So don't make any mistakes.'

She heard them grunt as they dragged the crate from the boat. Then their voices faded as they carried it into the tunnel.

It was now or never. The cliff face was pitted with holes and rough edges, but Holly picked her way back to Belinda as fast as she could. 'Quick!' she said. 'We haven't got long. Go for it.'

Together they hurried into the cove, where the boat was tied up to a post jammed into a crevice in the rock. It was dark in the shadow of the cliff, and they were working against time. Belinda's movements seemed unbearably slow and Holly couldn't curb her impatience.

'Hurry up,' she urged.

'I'm going as quick as I can.' Belinda had a thick, flexible pipe in her hand, and was running her fingers along it to see whether it went to the fuel tank. Holly saw her shake her head and bite her lip. She dug her hand once more into the tangle of cables and pipes. This time, she turned to Holly with a smile. 'Got it,' she said.

It took an age to cut through the thick plastic, but they were rewarded with the unmistakeable smell of petrol as the precious liquid drained away from the tank. 'Better get rid of the spare can too,' Belinda said. 'Then they can't go, even if they bind it up with tape.'

She grabbed the tin and threw it as far as she could into the sea. Then they began the long climb back.

They had just reached the cliff top when they heard the heavy rattle of the tractor starting up. Then the note of the engine deepened and they realised that it had begun to move. The two girls looked at each other and grinned. 'I wonder how long it will take them to realise that the trailer isn't with them?' Holly laughed. 'Come on, I'm dying to watch this.'

They ran down through the long grass, and heard a shout. *'Madre de Dios*! Come back. You have not the trailer!' In the light from the moon they saw the tractor chugging noisily towards the road. Way behind it was the figure of a man jumping up and down, waving his fists in the air.

The two girls put their hands over their mouths to stifle their giggles. The man raced after the tractor yelling a stream of Spanish. Then, abruptly, the tractor stopped. There was a momentary exchange of curses and the tractor began to reverse back to the trailer.

'Look!' Holly nudged her friend. Beyond the strip of marram grass they saw the dark outlines of a group of vehicles, waiting like silent hunters.

Suddenly, a whistle blew. Powerful searchlights lit up the area, and the place was blue with uniforms.

In the glare of light, Holly saw the Spaniard run towards the beach, but at a megaphone command to halt, he stopped abruptly and turned with his hands in the air. To Holly's surprise, the tractor still ambled forward, but as a burly policeman scrambled aboard and brought it to a halt, she realised that it was driverless.

So where was the driver? Where was Ian Clough? He mustn't get away. Breaking cover, Holly began to run towards the lights, waving her arms and shouting. Then she saw him . . .

He was running – a dark shadow dodging through the bracken. And behind him – another shadow, smaller . . . thinner . . . and unmistakeably Tracy.

'Get him, Tracy!' Holly yelled.

The leading figure hesitated for a moment, looked over his shoulder and as he did so, stumbled and nearly lost his balance.

Then the two girls were upon him – kicking, pummelling, and shouting for help all at the same time.

'Well done,' the Inspector said to the Mystery Club, when he came round to Carole's house the following day. The girls were sitting out on the terrace, sunbathing. They were all eating enormous bowls of raspberries and ice cream which Carole had dished up as a kind of thank-you present.

'I wish all our drug hauls were handed to us on a plate like that,' the Inspector continued. 'A million pounds' worth of cannabis in one hit. We got the whole gang this time too – thanks to you. Especially Ian Clough – the driver of the tractor. He might have got away but for you girls tackling him.'

'He wouldn't have got far,' Belinda said, popping a raspberry into her mouth. 'There was no fuel in the boat. I cut the pipe.'

The Inspector grinned. 'Well, let's say we'd have got him in the end, but you made our job a lot quicker. Would you like to know what happened to the rest of the gang?'

The girls nodded, and Belinda even put down her spoon for a split-second.

'One of our undercover men drove the truck to Sheffield this morning and picked up the contact buyer with no trouble at all. Martyn Hare and the couple at Wetherby's Farm were picked up late last night.'

'What about Mrs Wetherby?' Holly asked. 'Is she OK?'

The Inspector nodded. 'The doctor's been, and said she'll be fine in a few days' time.'

'I've got a nice surprise for her,' Carole added. 'I've got a buyer for the farm. A farmer's son, who wants to set up on his own. He's offering a very good price too. Better than I had hoped. Twice as much as Scarface was going to get it for.'

'What about the island?' Tracy asked.

'The Ministry of Defence have announced its decommission and given it over to Mr Bingley. He's going to set up a nature trust there for wildlife, and is looking round for someone to manage it.' The Inspector smiled. 'I wouldn't mind having a go at that myself. It would be a bit more peaceful than police work.'

He turned to go. 'Goodbye. Enjoy the rest of your holiday – short though it is. Our drug-running gang will be going on quite a different holiday, I'm afraid. A long, long holiday in prison.'

After Carole had seen the Inspector out, she came back into the garden. 'Well, this has been quite a week. You've crammed so much into so few days. I can't believe you will be going back home tomorrow. Now I know what your father means when he says that trouble follows you around.'

Holly laughed. 'It does, doesn't it? Still, at least it gives me plenty to write about for the school magazine. All I need now is the time to get it down on paper before the next mystery crops up.'

'And knowing you three,' her aunt said, 'that won't be long.'

MISCHIEF AT MIDNIGHT

by Fiona Kelly

Holly, Belinda and Tracy are back in the second
thrilling adventure in the Mystery Club series,
published by Knight Books.

Turn the page to read the first chapter . . .

1 A puzzling encounter

'What a gorgeous old cottage!' Holly Adams re-marked as the car drew up outside the last house in Goldenwood Lane.

Holly and her companion, Mrs Davies, a member of the Women's Volunteer Service, sat looking at the picturesque cottage.

'Yes,' Mrs Davies replied, turning to smile at Holly. 'The old couple, Mr and Mrs Benson, moved in a year or so ago.' She lowered her voice. 'The cottage is supposed to be haunted.'

Holly grinned, her intelligent grey eyes sparkling. 'You're kidding!' she exclaimed.

Mrs Davies shrugged. 'It's only a story, of course. When I visit them, Mr Benson always teases me about it. I think he quite frightens his wife with tales of strange noises and cold draughts, poor woman.'

'Well,' Holly said enthusiastically. 'I love ghost stories. I'll have to get Mr Benson to tell me all about it.'

'You might have a job even getting them to

answer the door I'm afraid,' Mrs Davies remarked, her voice full of regret. 'They're rather reluctant to open it to strangers these days. They used to be extremely friendly but they've grown suspicious lately. I did ask them last week if anything was wrong but they insisted they were all right. To be honest, it's all rather mysterious.'

Holly's ears pricked up. There was nothing she liked better than a good mystery.

'Maybe you could get them to talk to you,' Mrs Davies was saying. 'Tell you what they're so scared of.'

'What happens if they won't let me in?'

Mrs Davies smiled again. 'Don't worry, Holly. I'll stay here until I see them answer the door. Or would you like me to come in with you?'

Holly opened the car door. 'No, it's OK, thanks. I'm sure they'll see I'm only delivering their lunch. 'You'll pick me up in half an hour?'

'Yes. Thanks, Holly. I'm pleased you offered to help me out today. With two volunteers off sick, we're very short staffed.'

Holly went round to the rear of the car and took two warm plates of roast beef and Yorkshire pudding from the heated trolley. She waved to Mrs Davies then opened the rustic garden gate and marched up the front path.

She knocked smartly on the blue painted front door. 'Meals on wheels,' she called.

When there was no reply. Holly knocked again. The curtains were closed, so she wasn't able to peer through the window to see if anyone was inside.

How strange, Holly said to herself. *Either they've gone out or they really are too scared to open the door.*

Just then the curtains parted slightly and she could see someone peeping through the crack.

'Meals on wheels,' Holly called again loudly. 'I've brought your lunch.'

The curtains were drawn together again.

To Holly's relief she heard the sound of the door chain being unfastened and a bolt being drawn back. The door opened to reveal a short, elderly woman, white hair like candyfloss round her head. She peered at Holly suspiciously.

'Mrs Benson?' Holly enquired.

The elderly woman nodded. 'Yes.'

'I've brought your lunch, Mrs Benson,' Holly said brightly. 'It'll go cold soon.'

'You're not the usual person,' the woman said, frowning. 'Where's Mrs Davies?'

'I'm helping out today.' Holly turned her head slightly to indicate Mrs Davies waiting by the kerb. 'My name is Holly Adams. Mrs Davies is going to deliver a few other meals along the lane.'

The old lady peered at the car then called over her shoulder. 'It's all right, Arthur. It's only lunch.' She seemed to relax. She smiled uncertainly, then stood back for Holly to step inside. 'I'm sorry,' she said. 'We don't have many visitors and we're very wary of letting any strangers in at the moment.'

Behind her, Holly heard Mrs Benson lock and chain the door once more.

'Would you like to wait in the lounge while we eat our lunch?' Mrs Benson asked.'

'Yes, if that's OK. Mrs Davies won't be back for a while.'

Mrs Benson took the tray into the kitchen, then returned. She ushered Holly into the sitting-room.

'Thanks.' Holly sat down on the old, comfortable sofa. On the small oak coffee table there were a couple of magazines and a photograph album.

'Is it OK if I look at your photographs?' Holly asked. 'I love looking at people's pictures.'

'If you like,' Mrs Benson said. 'I'm afraid they're mostly of the cottage and the garden. A bit boring for a young person like yourself.'

On the first pages of the album were several pictures of a much younger man with short, fair hair. He was tall and bronzed and was dressed in jeans and a college sweatshirt. Holly could see he bore a distinct likeness to Mrs Benson.

Holly glanced around the room. It was small and cosy, with dark oak beams criss-crossing the ceiling. On the mantelpiece, in a cardboard mount, was another photograph of the young man.

Holly thumbed through the rest of the album then glanced at the magazines.

Mrs Benson came into the room with her husband.

'This is Holly Adams,' Mrs Benson said by way of introduction.

Holly stood up. 'Hello, Mr Benson,' she said shaking his hand. 'Thanks for letting me see your photos. They're great. Is that your son?' Holly indicated the photo on the mantelpiece.

Holly was puzzled at the secretive glance that passed between Mrs Benson and her husband.

'Er . . . yes, dear,' Mrs Benson answered. 'A friend must have taken the picture while he was on holiday. It just arrived out of the blue after – ' She broke off.

'After what?' Holly asked curiously.

'Just after he went away.' Mr Benson took the album from Holly.

'He doesn't live here then?'

Mrs Benson shook her head. 'No.'

Mr Benson sat down stiffly in his chair by the ingle-nook fireplace.

'Where does – ' Holly began.

'He lives away,' Mr Benson interrupted sharply with a frown.

'What school do you go to, dear?' Mrs Benson asked, clearly wanting to change the subject.

'Winifred Bowen-Davies,' Holly answered. Her

curiosity was immediately aroused. Holly was mad about mysteries of any kind and the Bensons' apparent reluctance to talk about their son seemed very odd. Most elderly people she knew were all too happy to talk about their children. Maybe they had quarrelled about something.

'Where do you live, Holly?' Mr Benson was asking.

Holly told the old couple about her family's cottage, located where the old and the new parts of Willow Dale met.

'We're renovating it,' she explained. 'But I'm afraid it's taking ages. We always seem to be in a mess. We lived in Highgate before.'

'We've lived in Willow Dale all our lives,' Mrs Benson was explaining. 'In fact David was born in the local hospital. He – '

Holly saw Mr Benson frown as his wife mentioned their son.

'But we only bought this cottage a year or so ago,' he interrupted quickly. 'We love it here. It's so peaceful. Or, it was until . . . '

Holly waited a minute for the old man to go on. 'Until what, Mr Benson? Has something happened to upset you?'

Mr Benson shook his head. 'No . . . no, of course not.'

'Mrs Davies told me the cottage is supposed to be haunted,' Holly said.

Holly saw Mrs Benson glance nervously at her husband. Maybe that was it. Maybe the old couple had been frightened by the ghost.

But to Holly's surprise a grin spread across Mr Benson's face. 'Now come on, June, you know it's only a story.' He looked at Holly. 'My wife believes in that sort of thing,' he added.

'You make me worse with all those stories you tell,' Mrs Benson said with a small smile.

'Well, you have to admit that room's always cold.'

'That's because it doesn't get any sun.' Mrs Benson turned to Holly. 'He really does make me nervous sometimes. It's bad enough as things are, without his stories to make it worse.'

'Make what worse?' Holly asked quickly.

'Nothing.' Mr Benson rose stiffly from his chair. 'Would you like to see the haunted room?'

'Oh, yes, please!'

'Come on then.' Mr Benson smiled.

Just at that moment there was a loud knock at the front door.

Holly saw Mrs Benson jump. Her hand flew to her mouth. 'Who can that be?' she exclaimed. It was clear the knock had scared her out of her wits.

Holly moved the curtain aside and looked out of the window. A tall, elegant woman with long dark hair and pale skin was standing on the doorstep, a letter in her hand. She wore a fashionable red suit with black high-heeled shoes. She was tapping her foot impatiently.

'It's a woman,' Holly said. 'She's got a letter for you by the looks of it.' She turned to see the old couple hurrying out of the room.

'Could you go please, Holly?' Mr Benson said. 'Tell her we're having our lunch.'

Before Holly could argue, the loud knock came again.

Holly hurried down the hall. She took the chain off the door and unlocked it.

On the doorstep, the woman looked startled for a moment. Then she smiled.

'Hello, dear. Can I possibly see Mr Benson, please?'

Although the woman was polite, Holly could see she was bristling with impatience.

'I'm afraid he's eating his lunch,' Holly said.

The woman stepped forward as if to push past. Holly stood her ground, putting her arm on the door frame to bar the woman's entrance.

'Perhaps I could give him a message?' she said firmly.

'I'm sorry, dear,' the woman said, 'but I really must see him. It's very important.' She smiled again. Her crimson lipstick was like a gash of blood across her face. 'Excuse me.'

Holly had no choice but to step back to allow her to pass.

'Hey!' Her protest came too late. The woman, seeing the front room empty, had disappeared into the kitchen. There, Holly heard voices.

'Well, here it is, Mr Benson. It's all in writing.'

Holly couldn't make out Mr Benson's reply.

Entering the kitchen, Holly saw the woman give Mr Benson the envelope.

'I warn you though,' the woman went on. 'We intend to take action if you don't comply with our wishes. I'd really like to prevent that if at all possible. I hate the thought of you and Mrs Benson being upset.'

'I've already given you my answer,' Mr Benson replied.

'Oh, come on,' the woman said in the same wheedling tone. Her dark eyes glittered. 'Surely you can see the sense in it?'

'No,' Mr Benson said emphatically. 'We don't see any sense in it. Now please leave.'

The woman shrugged. 'OK. But don't say I didn't warn you. Things could get very nasty if – '

'Just go!' Mr Benson shouted. Holly could see he was shaking with anger. Mrs Benson stood behind him, white-faced.

The woman shrugged. 'Very well,' she said icily. She spun on her heel and marched out.

Holly followed her to the front door.

'Thank you so much.' The woman looked Holly up and down. She frowned, her dark eyebrows almost meeting in the middle. 'You're not a relation of theirs, are you?' she asked.

'No – I'm working for the Volunteer Service.'

The woman raised her eyebrows. 'Pity. You might have persuaded them to see sense.' Then she turned and made off down the path. Holly watched her slam the gate and walk off down the lane, high heels clicking like castanets.

Holly shut the front door and went back into the kitchen. The Bensons were arguing.

'It's no good, Arthur,' Mrs Benson was saying. She was sitting at the kitchen table, her head in her hands. 'We'll have to do as she says.'

'Never!' Mr Benson said firmly. 'She can threaten us as much as she likes but we're not going to budge!'

'But, Arthur!' Mrs Benson looked up at her husband.

Mr Benson shook his head vehemently. 'No. You can say what you like, June, but we won't give in. I want to hear no more about it.'

Mrs Benson shrugged. 'You're just a stubborn old fool, Arthur.' She sighed. 'I do wish David was here. He'd sort things out for us.'

Mr Benson snorted. 'No chance of that!' he said bitterly.

'Is there anything I can do to help?' Holly asked.

The Bensons looked up, startled. Mr Benson

shook his head. 'No, dear.' He put the letter on the mantelpiece. Holly noticed the envelope had some kind of logo on the flap. It looked like the initials of some company or other. Mr Benson obviously wasn't going to open it while Holly was there. 'It's just a minor difference of opinion,' he assured her.

'Minor . . . ' Mrs Benson began, but she stopped when her husband frowned at her.

'Are you sure I can't help?' Holly said, sensing Mr Benson wasn't telling the truth.

Mrs Benson sniffed and managed a smile. She took out a lace-edged handkerchief and wiped her eyes. 'Yes, dear, quite sure. Let Arthur show you that wretched room before you go. I'll wash these plates up.'

Just then the sound of a car horn came from outside.

'Oh dear,' Holly exclaimed. She glanced out of the window. 'It's Mrs Davies. She must have finished delivering her meals. Can I come back another time to hear the story?'

'Of course, dear. Come whenever you like. We like having young people around.'

'I'm sorry I didn't manage to stop that woman coming in. I could see she upset you.'

Mr Benson shook his head. 'It's nothing, really.'

'Well, it didn't look like nothing,' Holly said emphatically. 'Look, I'll leave you my phone number in case you need help.' She wrote her number down on a pad by the telephone.

Whatever was wrong, Holly knew she wouldn't rest until she had got to the bottom of it. It looked as if a meeting of the Mystery Club was definitely called for!